The Complete Book

of the

Flower Fairies

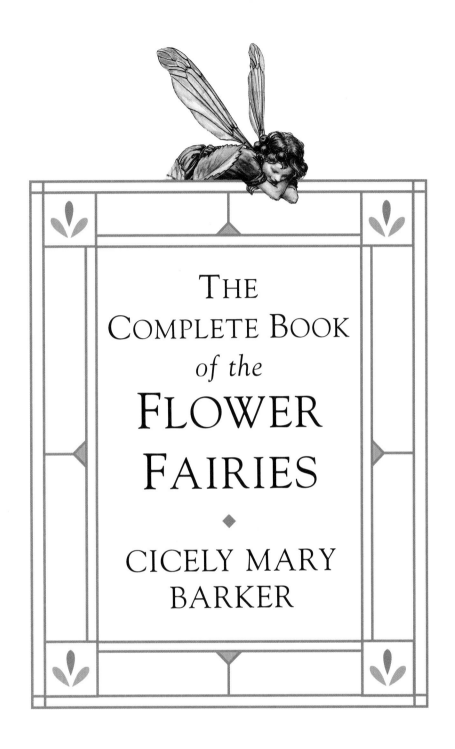

The Complete Book

of the

FLOWER FAIRIES

◆

CICELY MARY BARKER

FREDERICK WARNE

This edition published 2003 for Index Books Ltd

Published by the Penguin Group
Penguin Books Ltd, 80 Strand, London WC2R 0RL, England
Penguin Putnam Inc., 375 Hudson Street, New York, New York 10014, USA
Penguin Books Australia Ltd, 250 Camberwell Road, Camberwell, Victoria 3124, Australia
Penguin Books Canada Ltd, 10 Alcorn Avenue, Toronto, Ontario, Canada M4V 3B2
Penguin Books India (P) Ltd, 11 Community Centre, Panchsheel Park, New Delhi 110 017, India
Penguin Books (NZ) Ltd, Cnr Rosedale and Airborne Roads, Albany, Auckland, New Zealand
Penguin Books (South Africa) (Pty) Ltd, P O Box 9, Parklands 2121, South Africa

Penguin Books Ltd, Registered Offices: 80 Strand, London WC2R 0RL, England

Web site at: www.flowerfairies.com

First published by Frederick Warne 1996
15 17 19 20 18 16 14

ISBN 0 7232 4344 1

Printed and bound in Great Britain by William Clowes Limited, Beccles and London

CONTENTS

◆

Introduction

◆

Cicely Mary Barker was born in West Croydon, Surrey, on 28 June 1895. All her life she was physically frail and as a child suffered from epilepsy. Apart from bouts of illness, Cicely's childhood was happy and secure. The Barkers' were deeply religious and Cicely herself was a devout Christian who used art to express her spiritual beliefs. It was Cicely's father, an accomplished artist himself, who encouraged her artistic talent, enrolling her at Croydon Art Society when she was thirteen years old and paying for a correspondence course in art which she continued until 1919.

She was only sixteen when she had her first work accepted for publication as a set of postcards, and from that time she devoted her career to painting. She was greatly influenced by the Pre-Raphaelites and believed, as they did, in "truth to nature". In creating her Flower Fairies books, she painted from life whenever she could, sometimes enlisting the help of staff at Kew Gardens in finding and identifying plant specimens. The fairies too were painted from life, modelled on the children who attended her sister's nursery school. Cicely created the fairy costumes for the models to wear and fashioned miniature wings from twigs and gauze. When the paintings were complete, she wrote the accompanying poems.

The first of the Flower Fairies books, *Flower Fairies of the Spring*, was published in 1923, and was well received by the war-weary public, who were fascinated by fairies and charmed by her vision of innocence. In the foreword to *Flower Fairies of the Wayside*, the seventh book in the series, Cicely wrote: "So let me say quite plainly, that I have drawn all the plants and flowers very carefully, from real ones; and everything that I have said about them is as true as I could make it. But I have never seen a fairy; the fairies and all about them are just 'pretend'." This unique blend of accuracy and fantasy had by then established a popularity for the Flower Fairies books which endures to this day.

The Complete Book of the Flower Fairies is the largest ever collection of Cicely Mary Barker's fairy works. It contains each of her Flower Fairies books, using the material in the current editions, and it also includes a full-length children's story *The Fairy Necklaces*, and the fairy poems that she illustrated for *Old Rhymes for All Times*. These illustrations reveal the enormous artistic talent that has enabled Cicely Mary Barker's work to survive in a more aggressively modern age and to give pleasure to so many admirers.

Flower Fairies
✦ of the ✦
Spring

SPRING MAGIC

◆

The World is very old;
   But year by year
It groweth new again
   When buds appear.

The World is very old,
   And sometimes sad;
But when the daisies come
   The World is glad.

The World is very old;
   But every Spring
It groweth young again,
   And fairies sing.

◆ THE SONG OF ◆
THE CROCUS FAIRIES

Crocus of yellow, new and gay;
Mauve and purple, in brave array;
Crocus white
Like a cup of light,—
Hundreds of them are smiling up,
Each with a flame in its shining cup,
By the touch of the warm and welcome sun
Opened suddenly. Spring's begun!
Dance then, fairies, for joy, and sing
The song of the coming again of Spring.

◆ THE SONG OF ◆
THE CELANDINE FAIRY

Before the hawthorn leaves unfold,
Or buttercups put forth their gold,
By every sunny footpath shine
The stars of Lesser Celandine.

◆ THE SONG OF ◆
THE COLT'S-FOOT FAIRY

The winds of March are keen and cold;
I fear them not, for I am bold.

I wait not for my leaves to grow;
They follow after: they are slow.

My yellow blooms are brave and bright;
I greet the Spring with all my might.

◆ THE SONG OF ◆
THE DANDELION FAIRY

Here's the Dandelion's rhyme:
   See my leaves with tooth-like edges;
Blow my clocks to tell the time;
   See me flaunting by the hedges,
In the meadow, in the lane,
   Gay and naughty in the garden;
Pull me up—I grow again,
   Asking neither leave nor pardon.
Sillies, what are you about
   With your spades and hoes of iron?
You can never drive me out—
   Me, the dauntless Dandelion!

◆ THE SONG OF ◆
THE PRIMROSE FAIRY

The Primrose opens wide in spring;
   Her scent is sweet and good:
It smells of every happy thing
   In sunny lane and wood.
I have not half the skill to sing
   And praise her as I should.

She's dear to folk throughout the land;
   In her is nothing mean:
She freely spreads on every hand
   Her petals pale and clean.
And though she's neither proud nor grand,
   She is the Country Queen.

(This catkin is the
flower of the Sallow
Willow.)

◆ THE SONG OF ◆
THE WILLOW-CATKIN FAIRY

The people call me Palm, they do;
They call me Pussy-willow too.
And when I'm full in bloom, the bees
Come humming round my yellow trees.

The people trample round about
And spoil the little trees, and shout;
My shiny twigs are thin and brown:
The people pull and break them down.

To keep a Holy Feast, they say,
They take my pretty boughs away.
I should be glad—I should not mind—
If only people weren't unkind.

Oh, you may pick a piece, you may
(So dear and silky, soft and grey);
But if you're rough and greedy, why
You'll make the little fairies cry.

The Wind
-Flower
Fairy.

◆ THE SONG OF ◆
THE WINDFLOWER FAIRY

While human-folk slumber,
　　The fairies espy
Stars without number
　　Sprinkling the sky.

The Winter's long sleeping,
　　Like night-time, is done;
But day-stars are leaping
　　To welcome the sun.

Star-like they sprinkle
　　The wildwood with light;
Countless they twinkle—
　　The Windflowers white!

("Windflower" is another name for Wood Anemone.)

◆ THE SONG OF ◆
THE DAISY FAIRY

Come to me and play with me,
　　I'm the babies' flower;
Make a necklace gay with me,
Spend the whole long day with me,
　　Till the sunset hour.

I must say Good-night, you know,
　　Till tomorrow's playtime;
Close my petals tight, you know,
Shut the red and white, you know,
　　Sleeping till the daytime.

The Larch Fairy.

◆ THE SONG OF ◆ THE LARCH FAIRY

Sing a song of Larch trees
    Loved by fairy-folk;
Dark stands the pinewood,
    Bare stands the oak,
But the Larch is dressed and trimmed
    Fit for fairy-folk!

Sing a song of Larch trees,
    Sprays that swing aloft,
Pink tufts, and tassels
    Grass-green and soft:
All to please the little elves
    Singing songs aloft!

◆ THE SONG OF ◆ THE LADY'S-SMOCK FAIRY

Where the grass is damp and green,
Where the shallow streams are flowing,
Where the cowslip buds are showing,
    I am seen.

Dainty as a fairy's frock,
White or mauve, of elfin sewing,
'Tis the meadow-maiden growing—
    Lady's-smock.

The Lady's-Smock Fairy.

◆ THE SONG OF ◆
THE DOG-VIOLET FAIRY

The wren and robin hop around;
    The Primrose-maids my neighbours be;
The sun has warmed the mossy ground;
Where Spring has come, I too am found:
    The Cuckoo's call has wakened me!

(This is the Wild Hyacinth. The Bluebell of
Scotland is the Harebell.)

◆ THE SONG OF ◆
THE BLUEBELL FAIRY

My hundred thousand bells of blue,
    The splendour of the Spring,
They carpet all the woods anew
With royalty of sapphire hue;
The Primrose is the Queen, 'tis true.
    But surely I am King!
        Ah yes,
    The peerless Woodland King!

Loud, loud the thrushes sing their song;
    The bluebell woods are wide;
My stems are tall and straight and strong;
From ugly streets the children throng,
They gather armfuls, great and long,
    Then home they troop in pride—
        Ah yes,
    With laughter and with pride!

◆ THE SONG OF ◆
THE SPEEDWELL FAIRY

Clear blue are the skies;
    My petals are blue;
    As beautiful, too,
As bluest of eyes.

The heavens are high:
    By the field-path I grow
    Where wayfarers go,
And "Good speed," say I;

"See, here is a prize
    Of wonderful worth:
    A weed of the earth,
As blue as the skies!"

(There are many kinds of Speedwell:
this is the Germander.)

◆ THE SONG OF ◆
THE DAFFODIL FAIRY

I'm everyone's darling: the blackbird and
    starling
Are shouting about me from blossoming
    boughs;
For I, the Lent Lily, the Daffy-down-dilly,
Have heard through the country the call to
    arouse.
The orchards are ringing with voices
    a-singing
The praise of my petticoat, praise of my
    gown;
The children are playing, and hark! they are
    saying
That Daffy-down-dilly is come up to town!

◆ THE SONG OF ◆
THE STITCHWORT FAIRY

I am brittle-stemmed and slender,
But the grass is my defender.

On the banks where grass is long,
I can stand erect and strong.

All my mass of starry faces
Looking up from wayside places,

From the thick and tangled grass,
Gives you greeting as you pass.

(A prettier name for Stitchwort is Starwort,
but it is not so often used.)

◆ THE SONG OF ◆
THE HEART'S-EASE FAIRY

Like the richest velvet
    (I've heard the fairies tell)
Grow the handsome pansies
    within the garden wall;
When you praise their beauty,
    remember me as well—
Think of little Heart's-ease,
    the brother of them all!

Come away and seek me
    when the year is young,
Through the open ploughlands
    beyond the garden wall;
Many names are pretty
    and many songs are sung:
Mine—because I'm Heart's-ease—
    are prettiest of all!

(An old lady says that when she was a little girl the
children's name for the Heart's-ease or Wild Pansy
was Jump-up-and-kiss-me!)

The Heart'sease Fairy.

◆ THE SONG OF ◆
THE WOOD-SORREL FAIRY

In the wood the trees are tall,
    Up and up they tower;
You and I are very small—
    Fairy-child and flower.

Bracken stalks are shooting high,
    Far and far above us;
We are little, you and I,
    But the fairies love us.

(The Wild Arum has other names besides Lords-and-Ladies, such as Cuckoo-Pint and Jack-in-the-Pulpit.)

◆ THE SONG OF ◆ THE LORDS-AND-LADIES FAIRY

Here's the song of Lords-and-Ladies
   (in the damp and shade he grows):
I have neither bells nor petals,
   like the foxglove or the rose.
Through the length and breadth of England,
   many flowers you may see—
Petals, bells, and cups in plenty—
   but there's no one else like me.

In the hot-house dwells my kinsman,
   Arum-lily, white and fine;
I am not so tall and stately,
   but the quaintest hood is mine;
And my glossy leaves are handsome;
   I've a spike to make you stare;
And my berries are a glory in September.
   (BUT BEWARE!)

◆ THE SONG OF ◆ THE MAY FAIRY

My buds, they cluster small and green;
   The sunshine gaineth heat:
Soon shall the hawthorn tree be clothed
   As with a snowy sheet.

O magic sight, the hedge is white,
   My scent is very sweet;
And lo, where I am come indeed,
   The Spring and Summer meet.

The May Fairy.

The Cowslip Fairy.

◆ THE SONG OF ◆
THE COWSLIP FAIRY

The land is full of happy birds
And flocks of sheep and grazing herds.

I hear the songs of larks that fly
Above me in the breezy sky.

I hear the little lambkins bleat;
My honey-scent is rich and sweet.

Beneath the sun I dance and play
In April and in merry May.

The grass is green as green can be;
The children shout at sight of me.

Flower Fairies
• of the •
Summer

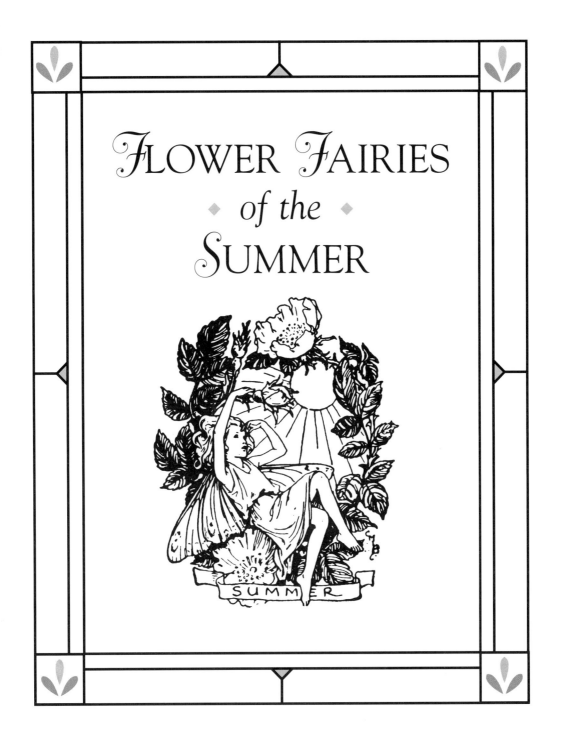

SPRING GOES, SUMMER COMES

◆

The little darling, Spring,
Has run away;
The sunshine grew too hot for her to stay.

She kissed her sister, Summer,
And she said:
"When I am gone, you must be queen
instead."

Now reigns the Lady Summer,
Round whose feet
A thousand fairies flock with blossoms sweet.

PLANTAIN AND MOON-DAISY DANCING TOGETHER,
ALL THROUGH THE BEAUTIFUL SUNSHINY WEATHER

◆ THE SONG OF ◆
THE BUTTERCUP FAIRY

'Tis I whom children love the best;
My wealth is all for them;
For them is set each glossy cup
Upon each sturdy stem.

O little playmates whom I love!
The sky is summer-blue,
And meadows full of buttercups
Are spread abroad for you.

◆ THE SONG OF ◆
THE POPPY FAIRY

The green wheat's a-growing,
    The lark sings on high;
In scarlet silk a-glowing,
    Here stand I.

The wheat's turning yellow,
    Ripening for sheaves;
I hear the little fellow
    Who scares the bird-thieves.

Now the harvest's ended,
    The wheat-field is bare;
But still, red and splendid,
    I am there.

◆ THE SONG OF ◆
THE HERB ROBERT FAIRY

Little Herb Robert,
　　Bright and small,
Peeps from the bank
　　Or the old stone wall.

Little Herb Robert,
　　His leaf turns red;
He's wild geranium,
　　So it is said.

◆ THE SONG OF ◆
THE BIRD'S-FOOT TREFOIL FAIRY

Here I dance in a dress like flames,
And laugh to think of my comical names.
Hoppetty hop, with nimble legs!
Some folks call me *Bacon and Eggs*!
While other people, it's really true,
Tell me I'm *Cuckoo's Stockings* too!
Over the hill I skip and prance;
I'm *Lady's Slipper,* and so I dance,
Not like a lady, grand and proud,
But to the grasshoppers' chirping loud.
My pods are shaped like a dicky's toes:
That is what *Bird's-Foot Trefoil* shows;
This is my name which grown-ups use,
But children may call me what they choose.

◆ THE SONG OF ◆
THE WHITE CLOVER FAIRY

I'm little White Clover, kind and clean;
Look at my threefold leaves so green;
Hark to the buzzing of hungry bees:
"Give us your honey, Clover, please!"

Yes, little bees, and welcome, too!
My honey is good, and meant for you!

◆ THE SONG OF ◆
THE HONEYSUCKLE FAIRY

The lane is deep, the bank is steep,
　The tangled hedge is high;
And clinging, twisting, up I creep,
　And climb towards the sky.
O Honeysuckle, mounting high!
O Woodbine, climbing to the sky!

The people in the lane below
　Look up and see me there,
Where I my honey-trumpets blow,
　Whose sweetness fills the air.
O Honeysuckle, waving there!
O Woodbine, scenting all the air!

◆THE SONG OF ◆
THE FORGET-ME-NOT FAIRY

So small, so blue, in grassy places
My flowers raise
Their tiny faces.

By streams my bigger sisters grow,
And smile in gardens,
In a row.

I've never seen a garden plot;
But though I'm small
Forget me not!

◆ THE SONG OF ◆
THE FOXGLOVE FAIRY

"Foxglove, Foxglove,
　What do you see?"
The cool green woodland,
　The fat velvet bee;
Hey, Mr Bumble,
　I've honey here for thee!

"Foxglove, Foxglove,
　What see you now?"
The soft summer moonlight
　On bracken, grass, and bough;
And all the fairies dancing
　As only they know how.

◆ THE SONG OF ◆
THE NIGHTSHADE FAIRY

My name is Nightshade, also Bittersweet;
    Ah, little folk, be wise!
Hide you your hands behind you when we meet,
    Turn you away your eyes.
My flowers you shall not pick, nor berries eat,
    For in them poison lies.

(Though this is so poisonous, it is not the Deadly Nightshade,
but the Woody Nightshade. The berries turn red a little later on.)

◆ THE SONG OF ◆
THE GREATER KNAPWEED FAIRY

Oh, please, little children, take note of my
    name:
To call me a thistle is really a shame:
I'm harmless old Knapweed, who grows
    on the chalk,
I never will prick you when out for your
    walk.

Yet I should be sorry, yes, sorry indeed,
To cut your small fingers and cause them
    to bleed;
So bid me Good Morning when out for
    your walk,
And mind how you pull at my very tough
    stalk.

(Sometimes this Knapweed is called Hardhead;
and he has a brother, the little Knapweed, whose
flower is not quite like this.)

◆ THE SONG OF ◆
THE HAREBELL FAIRY

O bells, on stems so thin and fine!
    No human ear
    Your sound can hear,
O lightly chiming bells of mine!

When dim and dewy twilight falls,
    Then comes the time
    When harebells chime
For fairy feasts and fairy balls.

They tinkle while the fairies play,
    With dance and song,
    The whole night long,
Till daybreak wakens, cold and grey,
And elfin music fades away.

(The Harebell is the Bluebell of Scotland.)

◆ THE SONG OF ◆
THE HEATHER FAIRY

"Ho, Heather, ho! From south to north
Spread now your royal purple forth!
Ho, jolly one! From east to west,
The moorland waiteth to be dressed!"

I come, I come! With footsteps sure
I run to clothe the waiting moor;
From heath to heath I leap and stride
To fling my bounty far and wide.

(The heather in the picture is bell heather, or heath; it is
different from the common heather which is also called ling.)

◆ THE SONG OF ◆
THE YARROW FAIRY

Among the harebells and the grass,
　　The grass all feathery with seed,
I dream, and see the people pass:
　　They pay me little heed.

And yet the children (so I think)
　　In spite of other flowers more dear,
Would miss my clusters white and pink,
　　If I should disappear.

(The Yarrow has another name, Milfoil, which means
Thousand Leaf; because her leaves are all made up of
very many tiny little leaves.)

◆ THE SONG OF ◆
THE TOADFLAX FAIRY

The children, the children,
　　they call me funny names,
They take me for their darling
　　and partner in their games;
They pinch my flowers' yellow mouths,
　　to open them and close,
Saying, *Snap-Dragon!*
　　　Toadflax!
　　　　or, *darling Bunny-Nose!*

The Toadflax, the Toadflax,
　　with lemon-coloured spikes,
With funny friendly faces
　　that everybody likes,
Upon the grassy hillside
　　and hedgerow bank it grows,
And it's *Snap-Dragon !*
　　　Toadflax!
　　　　and *darling Bunny-Nose!*

◆ THE SONG OF ◆
THE SCARLET PIMPERNEL FAIRY

By the furrowed fields I lie,
Calling to the passers-by:
"If the weather you would tell,
Look at Scarlet Pimpernel."

When the day is warm and fine,
I unfold these flowers of mine;
Ah, but you must look for rain
When I shut them up again!

Weather-glasses on the walls
Hang in wealthy people's halls:
Though I lie where cart-wheels pass
I'm the Poor Man's Weather-Glass!

◆ THE SONG OF ◆
THE SCABIOUS FAIRY

Like frilly cushions full of pins
For tiny dames and fairykins;

Or else like dancers decked with gems,
My flowers sway on slender stems.

They curtsey in the meadow grass,
And nod to butterflies who pass.

◆ THE SONG OF ◆
THE RAGWORT FAIRY

Now is the prime of Summer past,
　　Farewell she soon must say;
But yet my gold you may behold
　　By every grassy way.

And what though Autumn comes apace,
　　And brings a shorter day?
Still stand I here, your eyes to cheer,
　　In gallant gold array.

◆ THE SONG OF ◆
THE TRAVELLER'S JOY FAIRY

Traveller, traveller, tramping by
To the seaport town where the big ships lie,
See, I have built a shady bower
To shelter you from the sun or shower.
Rest for a bit, then on, my boy!
Luck go with you, and Traveller's Joy!

Traveller, traveller, tramping home
From foreign places beyond the foam,
See, I have hung out a white festoon
To greet the lad with the dusty shoon.
Somewhere a lass looks out for a boy:
Luck be with you, and Traveller's Joy!

(Traveller's Joy is Wild Clematis; and when the flowers are
over, it becomes a mass of silky fluff, and then
we call it Old-Man's-Beard.)

◆ THE SONG OF ◆
THE WILD ROSE FAIRY

I am the queen whom everybody knows:
     I am the English Rose;
As light and free as any Jenny Wren,
     As dear to Englishmen;
As joyous as a Robin Redbreast's tune,
     I scent the air of June;
My buds are rosy as a baby's cheek;
     I have one word to speak,
One word which is my secret and my song,
'Tis "England, England, England" all day long.

◆ THE SONG OF ◆
THE ROSE FAIRY

Best and dearest flower that grows,
Perfect both to see and smell;
Words can never, never tell
Half the beauty of a Rose—
Buds that open to disclose
Fold on fold of purest white,
Lovely pink, or red that glows
Deep, sweet-scented. What delight
     To be Fairy of the Rose!

Flower Fairies
• of the •
Autumn

With the nuts and berries they bring

AUTUMN

THE BERRY-QUEEN

◆

An elfin rout,
   With berries laden,
Throngs round about
   A merry maiden.

Red-gold her gown;
   Sun-tanned is she;
She wears a crown
   Of bryony.

The sweet Spring came,
   And lovely Summer:
Guess, then, her name—
   This latest-comer!

SEE ABOVE THE FAIRY'S HEAD, GUELDER-ROSE'S BERRIES RED.

◆ THE SONG OF ◆
THE MOUNTAIN ASH FAIRY

They thought me, once, a magic tree
    Of wondrous lucky charm,
And at the door they planted me
    To keep the house from harm.

They have no fear of witchcraft now,
    Yet here am I today;
I've hung my berries from the bough,
    And merrily I say:

"Come, all you blackbirds, bring your wives,
    Your sons and daughters too;
The finest banquet of your lives
    Is here prepared for you."

  (The Mountain Ash's other name is Rowan; and it used to
be called Witchentree and Witch-wood too.)

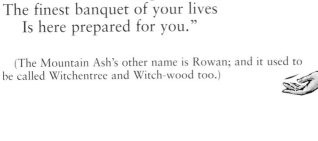

◆ THE SONG OF ◆
THE MICHAELMAS DAISY FAIRY

"Red Admiral, Red Admiral,
  I'm glad to see you here,
    Alighting on my daisies one by one!
I hope you like their flavour
  and although the Autumn's near,
    Are happy as you sit there in the sun?"

"I thank you very kindly, sir!
  Your daisies *are* so nice,
    So pretty and so plentiful are they;
The flavour of their honey, sir,
  it really does entice;
    I'd like to bring my brothers, if I may!"

"Friend butterfly, friend butterfly,
  go fetch them one and all!
    I'm waiting here to welcome every guest;
And tell them it is Michaelmas,
  and soon the leaves will fall,
    But *I* think Autumn sunshine is the best!"

◆ THE SONG OF ◆
THE WAYFARING TREE FAIRY

My shoots are tipped with buds as dusty-grey
As ancient pilgrims toiling on their way.

Like Thursday's child with far to go, I stand,
All ready for the road to Fairyland;

With hood, and bag, and shoes, my name to suit,
And in my hand my gorgeous-tinted fruit.

◆ THE SONG OF ◆
THE ROBIN'S PINCUSHION FAIRY

People come and look at me,
Asking who this rogue may be?
—Up to mischief, they suppose,
Perched upon the briar-rose.

I am nothing else at all
But a fuzzy-wuzzy ball,
Like a little bunch of flame;
I will tell you how I came:

First there came a naughty fly,
Pricked the rose, and made her cry;
Out I popped to see about it;
This is true, so do not doubt it!

(These berries do us no harm, though they don't taste very nice. Country people make wine from them; and boys make whistles from elder stems.)

◆ THE SONG OF ◆
THE ELDERBERRY FAIRY

Tread quietly:
O people, hush!
—For don't you see
A spotted thrush,
One thrush or two,
Or even three,
In every laden elder-tree?

They pull and lug,
They flap and push,
They peck and tug
To strip the bush;
They have forsaken
Snail and slug;
Unseen I watch them, safe and snug!

◆THE SONG OF◆
THE ACORN FAIRY

To English folk the mighty oak
   Is England's noblest tree;
Its hard-grained wood is strong and good
   As English hearts can be.
And would you know how oak-trees grow,
   The secret may be told:
You do but need to plant for seed
   One acorn in the mould;
For even so, long years ago,
   Were born the oaks of old.

(Cornel is another name
for Dogwood; and
Dogwood has nothing to
do with dogs. It used to
be Dag-wood, or
Dagger-wood, which,
with another name,
Prickwood, show that it
was used to make
sharp-pointed things.)

◆ THE SONG OF ◆
THE DOGWOOD FAIRY

I was a warrior,
   When, long ago,
Arrows of Dogwood
   Flew from the bow.
Passers-by, nowadays,
   Go up and down,
Not one remembering
   My old renown.

Yet when the Autumn sun
   Colours the trees,
Should you come seeking me,
   Know me by these:
Bronze leaves and crimson leaves,
   Soon to be shed;
Dark little berries,
   On stalks turning red.

◆ THE SONG OF ◆
THE HORSE CHESTNUT FAIRY

My conkers, they are shiny things,
    And things of mighty joy,
And they are like the wealth of kings
    To every little boy;
I see the upturned face of each
    Who stands around the tree:
He sees his treasure out of reach,
    But does not notice *me*.

For love of conkers bright and brown,
    He pelts the tree all day;
With stones and sticks he knocks them down,
    And thinks it jolly play.
But sometimes I, the elf, am hit
    Until I'm black and blue;
O laddies, only wait a bit,
    I'll shake them down to you!

◆ THE SONG OF ◆
THE BLACK BRYONY FAIRY

Bright and wild and beautiful
For the Autumn festival,
I will hang from tree to tree
Wreaths and ropes of Bryony,
To the glory and the praise
Of the sweet September days.

(There is nothing black to be seen about this Bryony, but
people do say it has a black root; and this may be true, but
you would need to dig it up to find out. It used
to be thought a cure for freckles.)

(You must believe the good
fairies, though the berries
look nice. This is the Woody
Nightshade, which has purple
and yellow flowers in the
summer.)

◆ THE SONG OF ◆
THE NIGHTSHADE BERRY FAIRY

"You see my berries, how they gleam and
     glow,
Clear ruby-red, and green, and orange-
     yellow;
Do they not tempt you, fairies, dangling so?"
  The fairies shake their heads and answer "No!
     You are a crafty fellow!"

"What, won't you try them? There is
     naught to pay!
Why should you think my berries poisoned
     things?
You fairies may look scared and fly away—
The children will believe me when I say
     My fruit is fruit for kings!"
  But all good fairies cry in anxious haste,
"*O children, do not taste!*"

◆ THE SONG OF ◆
THE BLACKBERRY FAIRY

My berries cluster black and thick
For rich and poor alike to pick.

I'll tear your dress, and cling, and tease,
And scratch your hands and arms and knees.

I'll stain your fingers and your face,
And then I'll laugh at your disgrace.

But when the bramble-jelly's made,
You'll find your trouble well repaid.

◆ THE SONG OF ◆
THE CRAB-APPLE FAIRY

Crab-apples, Crab-apples, out in the wood,
Little and bitter, yet little and good!
The apples in orchards, so rosy and fine,
Are children of wild little apples like mine.

The branches are laden, and droop to the
　　　ground;
The fairy-fruit falls in a circle around;
Now all you good children, come gather
　　　them up:
They'll make you sweet jelly to spread
　　　when you sup.

One little apple I'll catch for myself;
I'll stew it, and strain it, to store on a shelf
In four or five acorn-cups, locked with a key
In a cupboard of mine at the root of the tree.

◆ THE SONG OF ◆ THE ROSE HIP FAIRY

Cool dewy morning,
  Blue sky at noon,
White mist at evening,
  And large yellow moon;

Blackberries juicy
  For staining of lips;
And scarlet, O scarlet
  The Wild Rose Hips!

Gay as a gipsy
  All Autumn long,
Here on the hedge-top
  This is my song.

(This Bryony has other names—White Vine, Wild Vine, and Red-berried Bryony. It has tendrils to climb with, which Black Bryony has not, and its leaves and berries are quite different. They say its root is white, as the other's is black.)

◆ THE SONG OF ◆
THE WHITE BRYONY FAIRY

Have you seen at Autumn-time
        Fairy-folk adorning
All the hedge with necklaces,
        Early in the morning?
Green beads and red beads
        Threaded on a vine:
Is there any handiwork
        Prettier than mine?

◆ THE SONG OF ◆
THE HAZEL-NUT FAIRY

Slowly, slowly, growing
　　While I watched them well,
See, my nuts have ripened;
　　Now I've news to tell.
I will tell the Squirrel,
　　"Here's a store for you;
But, kind Sir, remember
　　The Nuthatch likes them too."

I will tell the Nuthatch,
　　"Now, Sir, you may come;
Choose your nuts and crack them,
　　But leave the children some."
I will tell the children,
　　"You may take your share;
Come and fill your pockets,
　　But leave a few to spare."

◆ THE SONG OF ◆
THE BEECHNUT FAIRY

O the great and happy Beech,
  Glorious and tall!
Changing with the changing months,
  Lovely in them all:

Lovely in the leafless time,
  Lovelier in green;
Loveliest with golden leaves
  And the sky between,

When the nuts are falling fast,
  Thrown by little me—
Tiny things to patter down
  From a forest tree!

(You may eat these.)

◆ THE SONG OF ◆
THE HAWTHORN FAIRY

These thorny branches bore the May
   So many months ago,
That when the scattered petals lay
   Like drifts of fallen snow,
   "This is the story's end," you said;
   But O, not half was told!
For see, my haws are here instead,
And hungry birdies shall be fed
   On these when days are cold.

◆ THE SONG OF ◆
THE PRIVET FAIRY

Here in the wayside hedge I stand,
And look across the open land;
Rejoicing thus, unclipped and free,
I think how you must envy me,
O garden Privet, prim and neat,
With tidy gravel at your feet!

(In early summer the Privet has spikes of very
strongly-scented white flowers.)

◆ THE SONG OF ◆
THE SLOE FAIRY

When Blackthorn blossoms leap to sight,
They deck the hedge with starry light,
    In early Spring
    When rough winds blow,
    Each promising
    A purple sloe.

And now is Autumn here, and lo,
The Blackthorn bears the purple sloe!
    But ah, how much
    Too sharp these plums,
    Until the touch
    Of Winter comes!

(The sloe is a wild plum. One bite will set your teeth on
edge until it has been mellowed by frost; but it is not poisonous.)

Flower Fairies
◆ of the ◆
Winter

◆ THE SONG OF ◆
THE SNOWDROP FAIRY

Deep sleeps the Winter,
    Cold, wet, and grey;
Surely all the world is dead;
    Spring is far away.
Wait! the world shall waken;
    It is not dead, for lo,
The Fair Maids of February
    Stand in the snow!

◆ THE SONG OF ◆
THE DEAD-NETTLE FAIRY

Through sun and rain, the country lane,
The field, the road, are my abode.
Though leaf and bud be splashed with mud,
Who cares? Not I!—I see the sky,
The kindly sun, the wayside fun
Of tramping folk who smoke and joke,
The bairns who heed my dusty weed
(No sting have I to make them cry),
And truth to tell, they love me well.
My brothers, White, and Yellow bright,
Are finer chaps than I, perhaps;
Who cares? Not I! So now good-bye.

◆ THE SONG OF ◆
THE SHEPHERD'S-PURSE FAIRY

Though I'm poor to human eyes
Really I am rich and wise.
Every tiny flower I shed
Leaves a heart-shaped purse instead.

In each purse is wealth indeed—
Every coin a living seed.
Sow the seed upon the earth—
Living plants shall spring to birth.

Silly people's purses hold
Lifeless silver, clinking gold;
But you cannot grow a pound
From a farthing in the ground.

Money may become a curse:
Give me then my Shepherd's Purse.

The Shepherd's-Purse Fairy.

The Groundsel Fairy.

◆ THE SONG OF ◆
THE GROUNDSEL FAIRY

If dicky-birds should buy and sell
In tiny markets, I can tell
    The way they'd spend their money.
They'd ask the price of cherries sweet,
They'd choose the pinkest worms for meat,
And common Groundsel for a treat,
    Though *you* might think it funny.

Love me not, or love me well;
That's the way they'd buy and sell.

◆ THE SONG OF ◆
THE OLD-MAN'S-BEARD FAIRY

This is where the little elves
Cuddle down to hide themselves;
Into fluffy beds they creep,
Say good-night, and go to sleep.

(Old-Man's Beard is Wild Clematis; its flowers are called
Traveller's Joy. This silky fluff belongs to the seeds.)

◆ THE SONG OF ◆
THE HAZEL-CATKIN FAIRY

Like little tails of little lambs,
   On leafless twigs my catkins swing;
They dingle-dangle merrily
   Before the wakening of Spring.

Beside the pollen-laden tails
   My tiny crimson tufts you see
The promise of the autumn nuts
   Upon the slender hazel tree.

While yet the woods lie grey and still
   I give my tidings: "Spring is near!"
One day the land shall leap to life
   With fairies calling: "Spring is HERE!"

The Hazel-Catkin Fairy.

◆ THE SONG OF ◆
THE BURDOCK FAIRY

Wee little hooks on each brown little bur,
(Mind where you're going, O Madam and Sir!)
How they will cling to your skirt-hem and stocking!
Hear how the Burdock is laughing and mocking:
Try to get rid of me, try as you will,
Shake me and scold me, I'll stick to you still,
      I'll stick to you still!

◆ THE SONG OF ◆
THE BOX TREE FAIRY

Have you seen the Box unclipped,
Never shaped and never snipped?
Often it's a garden hedge,
Just a narrow little edge;
Or in funny shapes it's cut,
And it's very pretty; *but*—

But, unclipped, it is a tree,
Growing as it likes to be;
And it has its blossoms too;
Tiny buds, the Winter through,
Wait to open in the Spring
In a scented yellow ring.

And among its leaves there play
Little blue-tits, brisk and gay.

◆ THE SONG OF ◆
THE RUSH-GRASS AND
COTTON-GRASS FAIRIES

Safe across the moorland
　　Travellers may go,
If they heed our warning—
　　We're the ones who know!

Let the footpath guide you—
　　You'll be safely led;
There is bog beside you
　　Where you cannot tread!

Mind where you are going!
　　If you turn aside
Where you see us growing,
　　Trouble will betide.

Keep you to the path, then!
　　Hark to what we say!
Else, into the quagmire
　　You will surely stray.

◆ THE SONG OF ◆
THE YEW FAIRY

Here, on the dark and solemn Yew,
  A marvel may be seen,
Where waxen berries, pink and new,
  Appear amid the green.

I sit a-dreaming in the tree,
  So old and yet so new;
One hundred years, or two, or three
  Are little to the Yew.

I think of bygone centuries,
  And seem to see anew
The archers face their enemies
  With bended bows of Yew.

◆ THE SONG OF ◆
THE LORDS-AND-LADIES FAIRY

Fairies, when you lose your way,
  From the dance returning,
In the darkest undergrowth
  See my candles burning!
These shall make the pathway plain
Homeward to your beds again.

(These are the berries of the Wild Arum, which has many
other names, and has a flower like a hood in the Spring.
The berries are not to be eaten.)

◆ THE SONG OF ◆
THE TOTTER-GRASS FAIRY

The leaves on the tree-tops
　　Dance in the breeze;
Totter-grass dances
　　And sways like the trees—

Shaking and quaking!
　　While through it there goes,
Dancing, a Fairy,
　　On lightest of toes.

(Totter-grass is also called Quaking-grass.)

◆ THE SONG OF ◆
THE WINTER JASMINE FAIRY

All through the Summer my leaves were green,
But never a flower of mine was seen;
Now Summer is gone, that was so gay,
And my little green leaves are shed away.
           In the grey of the year
           What cheer, what cheer?

The Winter is come, the cold winds blow;
I shall feel the frost and the drifting snow;
But the sun can shine in December too,
And this is the time of my gift to you.
           See here, see here,
           My flowers appear!

The swallows have flown beyond the sea,
But friendly Robin, he stays with me;
And little Tom-Tit, so busy and small,
Hops where the jasmine is thick on the wall;
           And we say: "Good cheer!
           We're here! We're here!"

(The cold days of March
are sometimes called
"Blackthorn Winter".)

◆ THE SONG OF ◆
THE BLACKTHORN FAIRY

The wind is cold, the Spring seems long
   a-waking;
    The woods are brown and bare;
Yet this is March: soon April will be making
    All things most sweet and fair.

See, even now, in hedge and thicket tangled,
    One brave and cheering sight:
The leafless branches of the Blackthorn,
    spangled
    With starry blossoms white!

◆ THE SONG OF ◆
THE PLANE TREE FAIRY

You will not find him in the wood,
    Nor in the country lane;
But in the city's parks and streets
    You'll see the Plane.

O turn your eyes from pavements grey,
    And look you up instead,
To where the Plane tree's pretty balls
    Hang overhead!

When he has shed his golden leaves,
    His balls will yet remain,
To deck the tree until the Spring
    Comes back again!

◆ THE SONG OF ◆
THE PINE TREE FAIRY

A tall, tall tree is the Pine tree,
    With its trunk of bright red-brown—
The red of the merry squirrels
    Who go scampering up and down.

There are cones on the tall, tall Pine tree,
    With its needles sharp and green;
Small seeds in the cones are hidden,
    And they ripen there unseen.

The elves play games with the squirrels
    At the top of the tall, tall tree,
Throwing cones for the squirrels to nibble—
    I wish I were there to see!

◆ THE SONG OF ◆
THE SPINDLE BERRY FAIRY

See the rosy-berried Spindle
All to sunset colours turning,
Till the thicket seems to kindle,
Just as though the trees were burning.
While my berries split and show
Orange-coloured seeds aglow,
One by one my leaves must fall:
Soon the wind will take them all.
Soon must fairies shut their eyes
For the Winter's hushabies;
But, before the Autumn goes,
Spindle turns to flame and rose!

◆ THE SONG OF ◆
THE HOLLY FAIRY

O, I am green in Winter-time,
   When other trees are brown;
Of all the trees (So saith the rhyme)
   The holly bears the crown.
December days are drawing near
   When I shall come to town,
And carol-boys go singing clear
Of all the trees (O hush and hear!)
   The holly bears the crown!

For who so well-beloved and merry
As the scarlet Holly Berry?

◆ THE SONG OF ◆
THE CHRISTMAS TREE FAIRY

The little Christmas Tree was born
    And dwelt in open air;
It did not guess how bright a dress
    Some day its boughs would wear;
Brown cones were all, it thought, a tall
    And grown-up Fir would bear.

O little Fir! Your forest home
    Is far and far away;
And here indoors these boughs of yours
    With coloured balls are gay,
With candle-light, and tinsel bright,
    For this is Christmas Day!

A dolly-fairy stands on top,
    Till children sleep; then she
(A live one now!) from bough to bough
    Goes gliding silently.
O magic sight, this joyous night!
    O laden, sparkling tree!

◆ THE SONG OF ◆
THE WINTER ACONITE FAIRY

Deep in the earth
I woke, I stirred.
I said: "Was that the Spring I heard?
For something called!"
"No, no," they said;
"Go back to sleep. Go back to bed.

"You're far too soon;
The world's too cold
For you, so small." So I was told.
But how could I
Go back to sleep?
I could not wait; I had to peep!

Up, up, I climbed,
And here am I.
How wide the earth! How great the sky!
O wintry world,
See me, awake!
Spring calls, and comes; 'tis no mistake.

Flower Fairies of the Garden

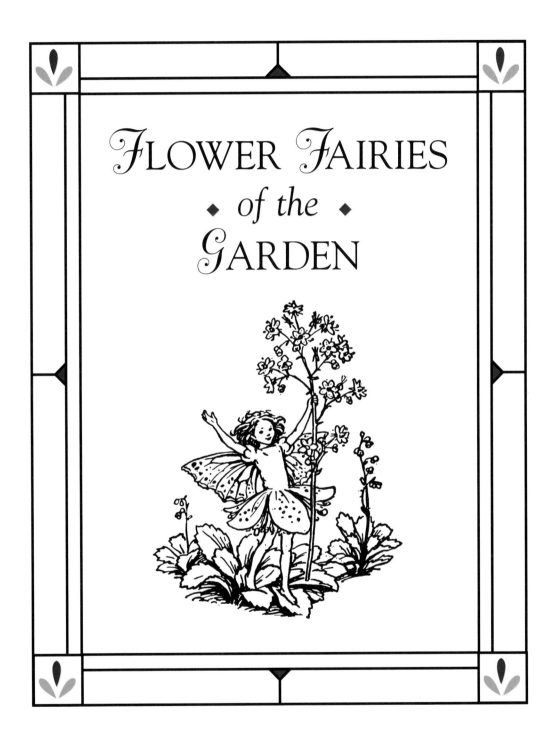

*W*HERE?

◆

Where are the fairies?
　　Where can we find them?
We've seen the fairy-rings
　　They leave behind them!

When they have danced all night,
　　Where do they go?
Lark, in the sky above,
　　Say, do you know?

Is it a secret
　　No one is telling?
*Why, in your garden
　　Surely they're dwelling!*

*No need for journeying,
　　Seeking afar:
Where there are flowers,
　　There fairies are!*

◆ THE SONG OF ◆
THE SCILLA FAIRY

"Scilla, Scilla, tell me true,
Why are you so very blue?"

Oh, I really cannot say
Why I'm made this lovely way!

I might know, if I were wise.
Yet—I've heard of seas and skies,

Where the blue is deeper far
Than our skies of Springtime are.

P'r'aps I'm here to let you see
What that Summer blue will be.

When you see it, think of me!

◆ THE SONG OF ◆
THE POLYANTHUS AND
GRAPE HYACINTH FAIRIES

"How do you do, Grape Hyacinth?
    How do you do?"
"Pleased to see *you*, Polyanthus,
    Pleased to see *you*,
With your stalk so straight
    and your colours so gay."
"Thank you, neighbour!
    I've heard good news today."

"What is the news, Polyanthus?
    What have you heard?"
"News of the joy of Spring,
    In the song of a bird!"
"Yes, Polyanthus, yes,
    I heard it too;
That's why I'm here,
    with my bells in spires of blue."

◆ THE SONG OF ◆
THE FORGET-ME-NOT FAIRY

Where do fairy babies lie
Till they're old enough to fly?
Here's a likely place, I think,
'Mid these flowers, blue and pink,
(Pink for girls and blue for boys:
Pretty things for babies' toys!)
Let us peep now, gently. Why,
Fairy baby, here you lie!

Kicking there, with no one by,
Baby dear, how good you lie!
All alone, but O, you're not—
You could *never* be—forgot!
O how glad I am I've found you,
With Forget-me-nots around you,
Blue, the colour of the sky!
Fairy baby, Hushaby!

◆ THE SONG OF ◆
THE PERIWINKLE FAIRY

In shady shrubby places,
Right early in the year,
I lift my flowers' faces—
O come and find them here!
My stems are thin and straying,
With leaves of glossy sheen,
The bare brown earth arraying,
For they are ever-green.
No great renown have I. Yet who
Does not love Periwinkle's blue?

(Some Periwinkles are more purple than these; and
every now and then you may find white ones.)

80

◆ THE SONG OF ◆
THE CORNFLOWER FAIRY

'Mid scarlet of poppies and gold of the corn,
In wide-spreading fields were the Cornflowers born;
But now I look round me, and what do I see?
That lilies and roses are neighbours to me!
There's a beautiful lawn, there are borders and beds,
Where all kinds of flowers raise delicate heads;
For this is a garden, and here, a Boy Blue,
I live and am merry the whole summer through.
My blue is the blue that I always have worn,
And still I remember the poppies and corn.

◆ THE SONG OF ◆
THE CANTERBURY BELL FAIRY

Bells that ring from ancient towers—
 Canterbury Bells—
Give their name to summer flowers—
 Canterbury Bells!
Do the flower-fairies, playing,
Know what those great bells are saying?
 Fairy, in your purple hat,
 Little fairy, tell us that!

"Naught I know of bells in towers—
 Canterbury Bells!
Mine are pink or purple flowers—
 Canterbury Bells!
When I set them all a-swaying,
Something, too, my bells are saying;
Can't you hear them—*ding-dong-ding*—
 Calling fairy-folk to sing?"

◆ THE SONG OF ◆
THE PINK FAIRIES

Early in the mornings,
    when children still are sleeping,
Or late, late at night-time,
    beneath the summer moon,
What are they doing,
    the busy fairy people?
Could you creep to spy them,
    in silent magic shoon,

You might learn a secret,
    among the garden borders,
Something never guessed at,
    that no one knows or thinks:
Snip, snip, snip, go busy fairy scissors,
Pinking out the edges
    of the petals of the Pinks!

Pink Pinks, white Pinks,
    double Pinks, and single,—
Look at them and see
    if it's not the truth I tell!
Why call them Pinks
    if they weren't pinked out by *someone*?
And what but fairy scissors
    could pink them out so well?

◆ THE SONG OF ◆
THE SHIRLEY POPPY FAIRY

We were all of us scarlet, and counted as
    weeds,
    When we grew in the fields with the corn;
Now, fall from your pepper-pots, wee little
    seeds,
    And lovelier things shall be born!

You shall sleep in the soil, and awaken next
    year;
    Your buds shall burst open; behold!
Soft-tinted and silken, shall petals appear,
    And then into Poppies unfold—

Like daintiest ladies, who dance and are gay,
    All frilly and pretty to see!
So I shake out the ripe little seeds, and I say:
    "Go, sleep, and awaken like me!"

(A clergyman, who was also a clever gardener, made these
many-coloured poppies out of the wild ones, and named them
after the village where he was the Vicar.)

◆ THE SONG OF ◆
THE TULIP FAIRY

Our stalks are very straight and tall,
    Our colours clear and bright;
Too many-hued to name them all—
    Red, yellow, pink, or white.

And some are splashed, and some, maybe,
    As dark as any plum.
From tulip-fields across the sea
    To England did we come.

We were a peaceful country's pride,
    And Holland is its name.
Now in your gardens we abide—
    And aren't you glad we came?

(But long, long ago, tulips
were brought from Persian gardens,
before there were any in Holland.)

◆ THE SONG OF ◆
THE SNAPDRAGON FAIRY

Into the Dragon's mouth he goes;
    Never afraid is he!
There's honey within for him, he knows,
    Clever old Bumble Bee!
The mouth snaps tight; he is lost to sight—
    How will he ever get out?
He's doing it backwards—nimbly too,
    Though he is somewhat stout!

Off to another mouth he goes;
    Never a rest has he;
He must fill his honey-bag full, he knows—
    Busy old Bumble Bee!
And Snapdragon's name is only a game—
    It isn't as fierce as it sounds;
The Snapdragon Elf is pleased as Punch
    When Bumble comes on his rounds!

◆ THE SONG OF ◆
THE GERANIUM FAIRY

Red, red, vermilion red,
With buds and blooms in a glorious head!
There isn't a flower, the wide world through,
That glows with a brighter scarlet hue.
Her name—Geranium—ev'ryone knows;
She's just as happy wherever she grows,
In an earthen pot or a garden bed—
    Red, red, vermilion red!

◆ THE SONG OF ◆
THE SWEET PEA FAIRIES

Here Sweet Peas are climbing;
   (Here's the Sweet Pea rhyme!)
Here are little tendrils,
   Helping them to climb.

Here are sweetest colours;
   Fragrance very sweet;
Here are silky pods of peas,
   Not for us to eat!

Here's a fairy sister,
   Trying on with care
Such a grand new bonnet
   For the baby there.

Does it suit you, Baby?
   Yes, I really think
Nothing's more becoming
   Than this pretty pink!

◆ THE SONG OF ◆
THE GAILLARDIA FAIRY

There once was a child in a garden,
  Who loved all my colours of flame,
The crimson and scarlet and yellow—
  But what was my name?

For *Gaillardia*'s hard to remember!
  She looked at my yellow and red,
And thought of the gold and the glory
  When the sun goes to bed;

And she troubled no more to remember,
  But gave me a splendid new name;
She spoke of my flowers as *Sunsets*—
  Then *you* do the same!

◆ THE SONG OF ◆
THE MARIGOLD FAIRY

Great Sun above me in the sky,
So golden, glorious, and high,
My petals, see, are golden too;
They shine, but cannot shine like you.

I scatter many seeds around;
And where they fall upon the ground,
More Marigolds will spring, more flowers
To open wide in sunny hours.

It is because I love you so,
I turn to watch you as you go;
Without your light, no joy could be.
Look down, great Sun, and shine on me!

◆ THE SONG OF ◆
THE LAVENDER FAIRY

"Lavender's blue, diddle diddle"—
    So goes the song;
All round her bush, diddle diddle,
    Butterflies throng;
(They love her well, diddle diddle,
    So do the bees;)
While she herself, diddle diddle,
    Sways in the breeze!

"Lavender's blue, diddle diddle,
    Lavender's green";
She'll scent the clothes, diddle diddle,
    Put away clean—
Clean from the wash, diddle diddle,
    Hanky and sheet;
Lavender's spikes, diddle diddle,
    Make them all sweet!

(The word "blue" was often used in old days
where we should say "purple" or "mauve".)

◆ THE SONG OF ◆
THE HELIOTROPE FAIRY

Heliotrope's my name; and why
People call me "Cherry Pie",
That I really do not know;
But perhaps they call me so,
'Cause I give them such a treat,
Just like something nice to eat.
For my scent—O come and smell it!
How can words describe or tell it?
And my buds and flowers, see,
Soft and rich and velvety—
Deepest purple first, that fades
To the palest lilac shades.
Well-beloved, I know, am I—
Heliotrope, or Cherry Pie!

◆ THE SONG OF ◆
THE CANDYTUFT FAIRY

Why am I "Candytuft"?
That I don't know!
Maybe the fairies
First called me so;
Maybe the children,
Just for a joke;
(I'm in the gardens
Of most little folk).

Look at my clusters!
See how they grow:
Some pink or purple,
Some white as snow;
Petals uneven,
Big ones and small;
Not very tufty—
No candy at all!

◆ THE SONG OF ◆
THE PHLOX FAIRY

August in the garden!
Now the cheerful Phlox
Makes one think of country-girls
Fresh in summer frocks.

There you see magenta,
Here is lovely white,
Mauve, and pink, and cherry-red—
Such a pleasant sight!

Smiling little fairy
Climbing up the stem,
Tell us which is prettiest?
She says, "All of them!"

◆ THE SONG OF ◆
THE NARCISSUS FAIRY

Brown bulbs were buried deep;
Now, from the kind old earth,
Out of the winter's sleep,
   Comes a new birth!

Flowers on stems that sway;
Flowers of snowy white;
Flowers as sweet as day,
   After the night.

So does Narcissus bring
Tidings most glad and plain:
"Winter's gone; here is Spring—
   Easter again!"

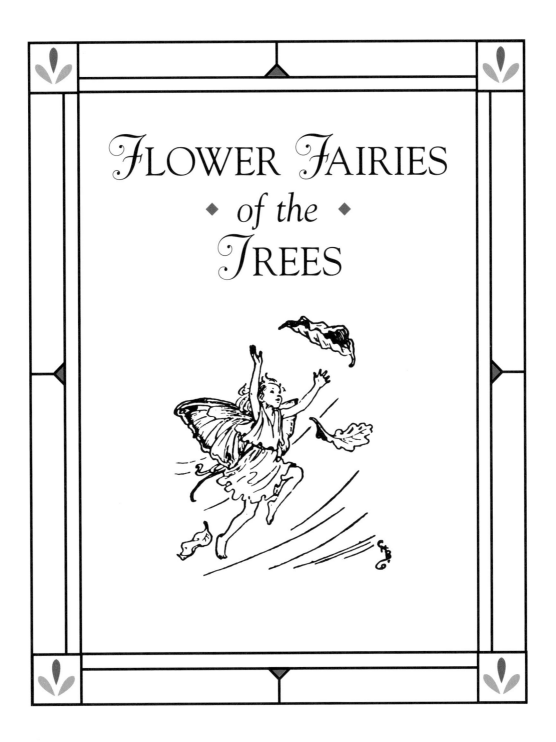

FLOWER FAIRIES
◆ *of the* ◆
TREES

ℒOOK UP!

◆

Look up, look up, at any tree!
There is so much for eyes to see:
Twigs, catkins, blossoms; and the blue
Of sky, most lovely, peeping through
Between the leaves, some large, some small,
Some green, some gold before their fall;
Fruits you can pick; fruits out of reach;
And little birds with twittering speech;
And, if you're quick enough, maybe
A laughing fairy in the tree!

◆ THE SONG OF ◆
THE PEAR BLOSSOM FAIRY

Sing, sing, sing, you blackbirds!
  Sing, you beautiful thrush!
It's Spring, Spring, Spring; so sing, sing, sing,
  From dawn till the stars say "hush".

See, see, see the blossom
  On the Pear Tree shining white!
It will fall like snow, but the pears will grow
  For people's and birds' delight.

Build, build, build, you chaffinch;
  Build, you robin and wren,
A safe warm nest where your eggs may rest;
  Then sit, sit, sit, little hen!

◆ THE SONG OF ◆
THE CHERRY TREE FAIRY

Cherries, a treat for the blackbirds;
  Cherries for girls and boys;
And there's never an elf in the treetops
  But cherries are what he enjoys!

Cherries in garden and orchard,
  Ripe and red in the sun;
And the merriest elf in the treetops
  Is the fortunate Cherry-tree one!

◆ THE SONG OF ◆
THE SILVER BIRCH FAIRY

There's a gentle tree with a satiny bark,
All silver-white, and upon it, dark,
Is many a crosswise line and mark—
    She's a tree there's no mistaking!
The Birch is this light and lovely tree,
And as light and lovely still is she
When the Summer's time has come to flee,
    As she was at Spring's awaking.

She has new Birch-catkins, small and tight,
Though the old ones scatter
    and take their flight,
And the little leaves, all yellow and bright,
    In the autumn winds are shaking.
And with fluttering wings
    and hands that cling,
The fairies play and the fairies swing
On the fine thin twigs,
    that will toss and spring
      With never a fear of breaking.

◆ THE SONG OF ◆
THE ALMOND BLOSSOM FAIRY

Joy! the Winter's nearly gone!
Soon will Spring come dancing on;
And, before her, here dance I,
Pink like sunrise in the sky.
Other lovely things will follow;
Soon will cuckoo come, and swallow;
Birds will sing and buds will burst,
But the Almond is the first!

◆ THE SONG OF ◆
THE WILD CHERRY BLOSSOM

In April when the woodland ways
Are all made glad and sweet
With primroses and violets
New-opened at your feet,
Look up and see
A fairy tree,
With blossoms white
In clusters light,
All set on stalks so slender,
With pinky leaves so tender.
O Cherry tree, wild Cherry tree!
You lovely, lovely thing to see!

◆ THE SONG OF ◆ THE WILLOW FAIRY

By the peaceful stream or the shady pool
I dip my leaves in the water cool.

Over the water I lean all day,
Where the sticklebacks and the minnows play.

I dance, I dance, when the breezes blow,
And dip my toes in the stream below.

◆ THE SONG OF ◆
THE BEECH TREE FAIRY

The trunks of Beeches are smooth and grey,
    Like tall straight pillars of stone
In great Cathedrals where people pray;
    Yet from tiny things they've grown.
About their roots is the moss; and wide
    Their branches spread, and high;
It seems to us, on the earth who bide,
    That their heads are in the sky.

And when Spring is here,
    and their leaves appear,
        With a silky fringe on each,
Nothing is seen so new and green
        As the new young green of Beech.
O the great grey Beech is young, is young,
    When, dangling soft and small,
Round balls of bloom from its twigs are hung,
    And the sun shines over all.

◆ THE SONG OF ◆
THE SYCAMORE FAIRY

Because my seeds have wings, you know,
    They fly away to earth;
And where they fall, why, there they grow—
    New Sycamores have birth!
Perhaps a score? Oh, hundreds more!
    Too many, people say!
And yet to me it's fun to see
    My winged seeds fly away.
(But first they must turn ripe and brown,
    And lose their flush of red;
And *then* they'll all go twirling down
    To earth, to find a bed.)

◆ THE SONG OF ◆
THE ELM TREE FAIRY

Soft and brown in Winter-time,
Dark and green in Summer's prime,
All their leaves a yellow haze
In the pleasant Autumn days—
See the lines of Elm trees stand
Keeping watch through all the land
Over lanes, and crops, and cows,
And the fields where Dobbin ploughs.
All day long, with listening ears,
Sits the Elm-tree Elf, and hears
Distant bell, and bleat, and bark,
Whistling boy, and singing lark.
Often on the topmost boughs
Many a rook has built a house;
Evening comes; and overhead,
Cawing, home they fly to bed.

◆ THE SONG OF ◆
THE ASH TREE FAIRY

Trunk and branches are smooth and grey;
    (Ash-grey, my honey!)
The buds of the Ash-tree, black are they;
    (And the days are long and sunny.)

The leaves make patterns against the sky,
    (Blue sky, my honey!)
And the keys in bunches hang on high;
    (To call them "keys" is funny!)

Each with its seed, the keys hang there,
    (Still there, my honey!)
When the leaves are gone
  and the woods are bare;
    (Short days may yet be sunny.)

(This is called the Black Poplar; but only, I think, because there is also a White Poplar, which has white leaves. The very tall thin Poplar is the Lombardy.)

◆ THE SONG OF ◆
THE POPLAR FAIRY

White fluff is drifting like snow round our feet;
　　Puff! it goes blowing
　　Away down the street.

Where does it come from? Look up and see!
　　There, from the Poplar!
　　Yes, from that tree!

Tassels of silky white fluffiness there
　　Hang among leaves
　　All a-shake in the air.

Fairies, you well may guess, use it to stuff
　　Pillows and cushions,
　　And play with it—puff!

◆ THE SONG OF ◆
THE LIME TREE FAIRY

Bees! bees! come to the trees
Where the Lime has hung her treasures;
Come, come, hover and hum;
Come and enjoy your pleasures!
The feast is ready, the guests are bidden;
Under the petals the honey is hidden;
Like pearls shine the drops of sweetness there,
And the scent of the Lime-flowers fills the air.
But soon these blossoms pretty and pale
Will all be gone; and the leaf-like sail
Will bear the little round fruits away;
So bees! bees! come while you may!

◆ THE SONG OF ◆
THE GUELDER ROSE

There are two little trees:
In the garden there grows
The one with the snowballs;
All children love *those*!

The other small tree
Not everyone knows,
With her blossoms spread flat—
Yet they're both Guelder Rose!

But the garden Guelder has nothing
    When her beautiful balls are shed;
While in Autumn her wild little sister
    Bears berries of ruby red!

◆ THE SONG OF ◆
THE ELDER FAIRY

When the days have grown in length,
When the sun has greater power,
Shining in his noonday strength;
When the Elder Tree's in flower;
When each shady kind of place
By the stream and up the lane,
Shows its mass of creamy lace—
Summer's really come again!

◆ THE SONG OF ◆
THE LILAC FAIRY

White May is flowering,
　　Red May beside;
Laburnum is showering
　　Gold far and wide;
But *I* sing of Lilac,
　　The dearly-loved Lilac,
Lilac, in Maytime
　　A joy and a pride!

I love her so much
　　That I never can tell
If she's sweeter to look at,
　　Or sweeter to smell.

(After the flowers, the Laburnum has pods with what look like tiny green peas in them; but it is best not to play with them, and they must never, never be eaten, as they are poisonous.)

◆ THE SONG OF ◆
THE LABURNUM FAIRY

All Laburnum's
Yellow flowers
Hanging thick
In happy showers,—
Look at them!
The reason's plain
Why folks call them
"Golden Rain"!
"Golden Chains"
They call them too,
Swinging there
Against the blue.

◆ THE SONG OF ◆
THE ALDER FAIRY

By the lake or river-side
   Where the Alders dwell,
In the Autumn may be spied
   Baby catkins; cones beside—
Old and new as well.
   Seasons come and seasons go;
That's the tale they tell!

After Autumn, Winter's cold
   Leads us to the Spring;
And, before the leaves unfold,
On the Alder you'll behold,
   Crimson catkins swing!
They are making ready now:
   That's the song I sing!

◆ THE SONG OF ◆
THE SWEET CHESTNUT FAIRY

Chestnuts, sweet Chestnuts,
  To pick up and eat,
Or keep until Winter,
  When, hot, they're a treat!

Like hedgehogs, their shells
  Are prickly outside;
But silky within,
  Where the little nuts hide,

Till the shell is split open,
  And, shiny and fat,
The Chestnut appears;
  Says the Fairy: "How's *that*?"

111

◆ THE SONG OF ◆
THE MULBERRY FAIRY

"Here we go round the Mulberry bush!"
You remember the rhyme—oh yes!
But which of you know
How Mulberries grow
On the slender branches, drooping low?
Not many of you, I guess.

Someone goes round the Mulberry bush
When nobody's there to see;
He takes the best
And he leaves the rest,
From top to toe like a Mulberry drest:
This fat little fairy's he!

Flower Fairies
of the
Wayside

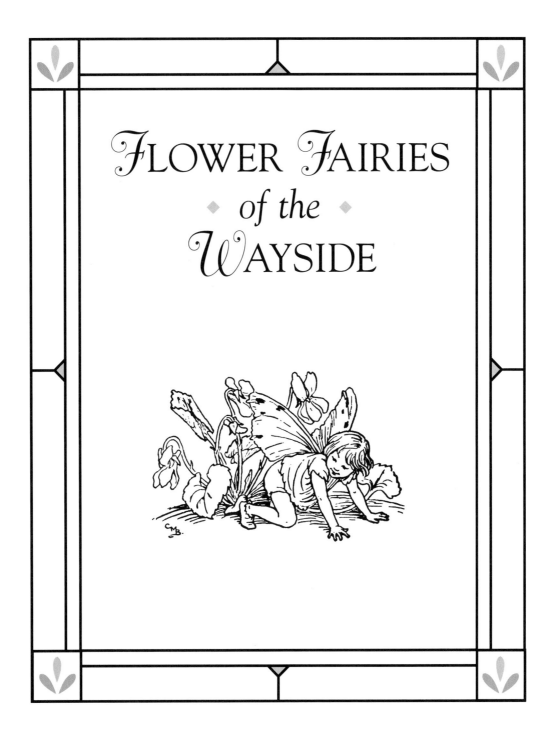

OPEN YOUR EYES!

◆

To shop, and school, to work and play,
The busy people pass all day;
They hurry, hurry, to and fro,
And hardly notice as they go
The wayside flowers, known so well,
Whose names so few of them can tell.

They never think of fairy-folk
Who may be hiding for a joke!

O, if these people understood
What's to be found by field and wood;
What fairy secrets are made plain
By any footpath, road, or lane—
They'd go with open eyes, and *look*,
(As you will, when you've read this book)
And then at least they'd learn to see
How pretty common things can be!

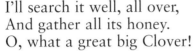

◆ THE SONG OF ◆
THE RED CLOVER FAIRY

The Fairy: O, what a great big bee
                Has come to visit me!
                He's come to find my honey.
                O, what a great big bee!

The Bee: O, what a great big Clover!
                I'll search it well, all over,
                And gather all its honey.
                O, what a great big Clover!

◆ THE SONG OF ◆
THE GREATER CELANDINE FAIRY

You come with the Spring,
    O swallow on high!
You come with the Spring,
    And so do I.

Your nest, I know,
    Is under the eaves;
While far below
    Are my flowers and leaves.

Yet, to and fro
    As you dart and fly,
You swoop so low
    That you brush me by!

I come with the Spring;
    The wall is my home;
I come with the Spring
    When the swallows come.

(The name "Celandine" comes from the Greek word for
"swallow", and this celandine used sometimes to be called
"swallow-wort". It has orange-coloured juice in its stems,
and is no relation to the Lesser Celandine, which is in *Flower
Fairies of the Spring;* but it is a relation of the Horned Poppy,
which you will find further on in this book.)

◆ THE SONG OF ◆
THE JACK-BY-THE-HEDGE FAIRY

"'Morning, Sir, and how-d'ye-do?
   'Morning, pretty lady!"
That is Jack saluting you,
   Where the lane is shady.

Don't you know him? Straight and tall—
   Taller than the nettles;
Large and light his leaves; and small
   Are his buds and petals.

Small and white, with petals four,
   See his flowers growing!
If you never knew before,
   There is Jack for knowing!

(Jack-by-the-hedge is also called Garlic Mustard,
and Sauce Alone.)

◆ THE SONG OF ◆
THE GROUND IVY FAIRY

In Spring he is found;
He creeps on the ground;
But someone's to blame
For the rest of his name—
For Ivy he's *not*!
Oh dear, what a lot
Of muddles we make!
It's quite a mistake,
And really a pity
Because he's so pretty;
He deserves a nice name—
Yes, *someone's* to blame!

(But he has some other names, which we do not hear very
often; here are four of them: Robin-run-up-the-dyke,
Runnadyke, Run-away-Jack, Creeping Charlie.)

(Another name for this Willow-Herb is "Fireweed", because of its way of growing where there have been heath or forest fires.)

◆ THE SONG OF ◆
THE ROSE-BAY
WILLOW-HERB FAIRY

On the breeze my fluff is blown;
So my airy seeds are sown.

Where the earth is burnt and sad,
I will come to make it glad.

All forlorn and ruined places,
All neglected empty spaces,

I can cover—only think!—
With a mass of rosy pink.

Burst then, seed-pods; breezes, blow!
Far and wide my seeds shall go!

◆ THE SONG OF ◆
THE WHITE BINDWEED FAIRY

O long long stems that twine!
O buds, so neatly furled!
O great white bells of mine,
(None purer in the world)
Each lasting but one day!
O leafy garlands, hung
In wreaths beside the way—
Well may your praise be sung!

(But this Bindweed, which is a big sister to the little pink
Field Convolvulus, is not good to have in gardens,
though it is so beautiful; because it winds around
other plants and trees. One of its names is "Hedge
Strangler". Morning Glories are a garden
kind of Convolvulus.)

◆ THE SONG OF ◆
THE BLACK MEDICK FAIRIES

"Why are we called 'Black', sister,
  When we've yellow flowers?"
"I will show you why, brother:
  See these seeds of ours?
Very soon each tiny seed
  Will be turning black indeed!"

◆ THE SONG OF ◆
THE RED CAMPION FAIRY

Here's a cheerful somebody,
  By the woodland's edge;
Campion the many-named,
  Robin-in-the-hedge.

Coming when the bluebells come,
  When they're gone, he stays,
(Round Robin, Red Robin)
  All the summer days.

Soldiers' Buttons, Robin Flower,
  In the lane or wood;
Robin Redbreast, Red Jack,
  Yes, and Robin Hood!

◆ THE SONG OF ◆
THE FUMITORY FAIRY

Given me hundreds of years ago,
My name has a meaning you shall know:
It means, in the speech of the bygone folk,
"Smoke of the Earth" —a soft green smoke!

A wonderful plant to them I seemed;
Strange indeed were the dreams they dreamed,
Partly fancy and partly true,
About "Fumiter" and the way it grew.

Where men have ploughed
    or have dug the ground,
Still, with my rosy flowers, I'm found;
Known and prized by the bygone folk
As "Smoke of the Earth" —
    a soft green smoke!

(The name "Fumitory" was "Fumiter" 300 years ago; and long
  before that, "Fume Terre", which is the French name, still, for
  the plant. "Fume" means "smoke", "terre" means "earth".)

◆ THE SONG OF ◆
THE SOW THISTLE FAIRY

I have handsome leaves, and my stalk is tall,
    And my flowers are prettily yellow;
Yet nobody thinks me nice at all:
    They think me a tiresome fellow—
        An ugly weed
        And a rogue indeed;
    For wherever I happen to spy,
        As I look around,
        That they've dug their ground,
    I say to my seeds "Go, fly!"

And because I am found
On the nice soft ground,
A trespassing weed am I!

(But I have heard that Sow Thistle is good rabbit-food, so
  perhaps it is not so useless as most people think.)

123

◆ THE SONG OF ◆
THE BEE ORCHIS FAIRY

In the grass o' the bank,
  by the side o' the way,
    Where your feet may stray
    On your luckiest day,
There's a sight most rare
  that your eyes may see:
A beautiful orchis that looks like a bee!
A velvety bee, with a proud little elf,
Who looks like the wonderful
  orchis himself—
    In the grass o' the hill,
    Not often, but still
    Just once in a way
    On your luckiest day!

◆ THE SONG OF ◆
THE SELF-HEAL FAIRY

When little elves have cut themselves,
  Or Mouse has hurt her tail,
Or Froggie's arm has come to harm,
  This herb will never fail.
The Fairy's skill can cure each ill
  And soothe the sorest pain;
She'll bathe, and bind, and soon they'll find
  That they are well again.

(This plant was a famous herb of healing in old days, as you
  can tell by the names it was given—Self-Heal,
  All-Heal, and others. It is also called Prunella.)

(There are some other kinds of Plantain besides this. The one with wide leaves, and tall spikes of seed which canaries enjoy, is Greater Plantain.)

◆ THE SONG OF ◆
THE RIBWORT PLANTAIN FAIRY

Hullo, Snailey-O!
How's the world with *you*?
Put your little horns out;
Tell me how you do?
There's rain, and dust, and sunshine,
Where carts go creaking by;
You like it wet, Snailey;
I like it dry!

Hey ho, Snailey-O,
I'll whistle you a tune!
I'm merry in September
As e'er I am in June.
By any stony roadside
Wherever you may roam,
All the summer through, Snailey,
Plantain's at home!

◆ THE SONG OF ◆
THE AGRIMONY FAIRIES

Spikes of yellow flowers,
  All along the lane;
When the petals vanish,
  Burrs of red remain.

First the spike of flowers,
  Then the spike of burrs;
Carry them like soldiers,
  Smartly, little sirs!

◆ THE SONG OF ◆
THE CHICORY FAIRY

By the white cart-road,
   Dusty and dry,
Look! there is Chicory,
   Blue as the sky!

Or, where the footpath
   Goes through the corn,
See her bright flowers,
   Each one new-born!

Though they fade quickly,
   O, have no sorrow!
There will be others
   New-born tomorrow!

(Chicory is also called Succory.)

◆ THE SONG OF ◆
THE HORNED POPPY FAIRY

These are the things I love and know:
The sound of the waves, the sight of the sea;
The great wide shore when the tide is low;
Where there's salt in the air, it's home to me—
With my petals of gold—the home for me!

The waves come up and cover the sand,
Then turn at the pebbly slope of the beach;
I feel the spray of them, where I stand,
Safe and happy, beyond their reach—
With my marvellous horns—
    beyond their reach!

◆ THE SONG OF ◆
THE STORK'S-BILL FAIRY

"Good morning, Mr Grasshopper!
    Please stay and talk a bit!"
"Why yes, you pretty Fairy;
    Upon this grass I'll sit.
And let us ask some riddles;
    They're better fun than chat:
Why am I like the Stork's-bill?
    Come, can you answer *that?*"

"Oh no, you clever Grasshopper!
    I fear I am a dunce;
I cannot guess the answer—
    I give it up at once!"
"When children think they've caught me,
    I'm gone, with leap and hop;
And when they gather Stork's-bill,
    Why, all the petals drop!"

(The Stork's-bill gets her name from the long seed-pod,
which looks like a stork's beak or bill. Others of her
family are called Crane's-bills.)

◆ THE SONG OF ◆
THE JACK-GO-TO-BED-
AT-NOON FAIRY

I'll be asleep by noon!
Though bedtime comes so soon,
   I'm busy too.
Twelve puffs!—and then from sight
I shut my flowers tight;
Only by morning light
   They're seen by you.

Then, on some day of sun,
They'll open wide, each one,
   As something new!
Shepherd, who minds his flock,
Calls it a Shepherd's Clock,
Though it can't say "tick-tock"
   As others do!

(Another of Jack's names, besides
Shepherd's Clock is Goat's Beard.)

◆ THE SONG OF ◆
THE TANSY FAIRY

In busy kitchens, in olden days,
Tansy was used in a score of ways;
Chopped and pounded,
   when cooks would make
Tansy puddings and tansy cake,
Tansy posset, or tansy tea;
Physic or flavouring tansy'd be.
       People who know
       Have told me so!

That is my tale of the past; today,
Still I'm here by the King's Highway,
Where the air from the fields
   is fresh and sweet,
With my fine-cut leaves and my flowers neat.
Were ever such button-like flowers seen—
Yellow, for elfin coats of green?
       Three in a row—
       I stitch them so!

A
FLOWER FAIRY
ALPHABET

Apple Blossom

◆ THE SONG OF ◆
THE APPLE BLOSSOM FAIRIES

Up in the tree we see you, blossom-babies,
      All pink and white;
We think there must be fairies to protect you
      From frost and blight,
Until, some windy day, in drifts of petals,
      You take your flight.

You'll fly away! But if we wait with patience,
      Some day we'll find
Here, in your place, full-grown and ripe, the apples
      You left behind—
A goodly gift indeed, from blossom-babies
      To human-kind!

◆ THE SONG OF ◆
THE BUGLE FAIRY

At the edge of the woodland
Where good fairies dwell,
Stands, on the look-out,
A brave sentinel.

At the call of his bugle
Out the elves run,
Ready for anything,
Danger, or fun,
Hunting, or warfare,
By moonshine or sun.

With bluebells and campions
The woodlands are gay,
Where bronzy-leaved Bugle
Keeps watch night and day.

Bugle

Columbine

◆ THE SONG OF ◆
THE COLUMBINE FAIRY

Who shall the chosen fairy be
    For letter C?
There's Candytuft, and Cornflower blue,
Campanula and Crocus too,
Chrysanthemum so bold and fine,
And pretty dancing Columbine.

Yes, Columbine! The choice is she;
    And with her, see,
An elfin piper, piping sweet
A little tune for those light feet
That dance among the leaves and flowers
In *someone's* garden.
        (Is it ours?)

Double Daisy

◆ THE SONG OF ◆
THE DOUBLE DAISY FAIRY

Dahlias and Delphiniums,
  you're too tall for me;
Isn't there a *little* flower
  I can choose for D?

In the smallest flower-bed
Double Daisy lifts his head,
With a smile to greet the sun,
You, and me, and everyone.

Crimson Daisy, now I see
You're the little lad for me!

Eyebright

◆ THE SONG OF ◆
THE EYEBRIGHT FAIRY

Eyebright for letter E:
Where shall we look for him?
Bright eyes we'll need to see
Someone so small as he.
Where is the nook for him?

Look on the hillside bare,
Nibbled by bunnies;
Harebells and thyme are there,
All in the open air
Where the great sun is.

There in the turf is he,
(No sheltered nook for him!)
Eyebright for letter E,
Saying, "Please, this is me!"
That's where to look for him.

◆ THE SONG OF ◆
THE FUCHSIA FAIRY

Fuchsia is a dancer
Dancing on her toes,
Clad in red and purple,
By a cottage wall;
Sometimes in a greenhouse,
In frilly white and rose,
Dressed in her best for the fairies' evening ball!

(This is the little out-door Fuchsia.)

Fuchsia

G

Gorse

◆ THE SONG OF ◆
THE GORSE FAIRIES

"When gorse is out of blossom,"
   (Its prickles bare of gold)
"Then kissing's out of fashion,"
   Said country-folk of old.
Now Gorse is in its glory
   In May when skies are blue,
But when its time is over,
   Whatever shall we do?

O dreary would the world be,
   With everyone grown cold—
Forlorn as prickly bushes
   Without their fairy gold!
But this will never happen:
   At every time of year
You'll find one bit of blossom—
   A kiss from someone dear!

Herb Twopence

(Hyacinth, Heliotrope, Honeysuckle, and Hollyhock,
are some more flowers beginning with H.)

◆ THE SONG OF ◆
THE HERB TWOPENCE FAIRY

Have you pennies? I have many:
    Each round leaf of mine's a penny,
Two and two along the stem—
    Such a business, counting them!
(While I talk, and while you listen,
    Notice how the green leaves glisten,
Also every flower-cup:
    Don't I keep them polished up?)

Have you *one* name? I have many:
    "Wandering Sailor", "Creeping Jenny",
"Money-wort", and of the rest
    "Strings of Sovereigns" is the best,
(That's my yellow flowers, you see.)
    "Meadow Runagates" is me,
And "Herb Twopence". Tell me which
    Show I stray, and show I'm rich?

◆ THE SONG OF ◆
THE IRIS FAIRY

I am Iris: I'm the daughter
Of the marshland and the water.
Looking down, I see the gleam
Of the clear and peaceful stream;
Water-lilies large and fair
With their leaves are floating there;
All the water-world I see,
And my own face smiles at me!

(This is the wild Iris.)

Iris

Jasmine

◆ THE SONG OF ◆
THE JASMINE FAIRY

In heat of summer days
With sunshine all ablaze,
Here, here are cool green bowers,
Starry with Jasmine flowers;
Sweet-scented, like a dream
Of Fairyland they seem.

And when the long hot day
At length has worn away,
And twilight deepens, till
The darkness comes—then, still,
The glimmering Jasmine white
Gives fragrance to the night.

◆ THE SONG OF ◆
THE KINGCUP FAIRY

Golden King of marsh and swamp,
Reigning in your springtime pomp,
Hear the little elves you've found
Trespassing on royal ground:—

"Please, your Kingship, we were told
Of your shining cups of gold;
So we came here, just to see—
Not to rob your Majesty!"

Golden Kingcup, well I know
You will smile and let them go!
Yet let human folk beware
How they thieve and trespass there:

Kingcup-laden, they may lose
In the swamp their boots and shoes!

Kingcup

Lily-of-the-Valley

◆ THE SONG OF ◆
THE LILY-OF-THE-VALLEY FAIRY

Gentle fairies, hush your singing:
Can you hear my white bells ringing,
Ringing as from far away?
Who can tell me what they say?

Little snowy bells out-springing
From the stem and softly ringing—
Tell they of a country where
Everything is good and fair?

Lovely, lovely things for L!
Lilac, Lavender as well;
And, more sweet than rhyming tells,
Lily-of-the-Valley's bells.

(Lily-of-the-Valley is sometimes called Ladders to Heaven.)

◆ THE SONG OF ◆
THE MALLOW FAIRY

I am Mallow; here sit I
Watching all the passers-by.
Though my leaves are torn and tattered,
Dust-besprinkled, mud-bespattered,
See, my seeds are fairy cheeses,
Freshest, finest, fairy cheeses!
These are what an elf will munch
For his supper or his lunch.
Fairy housewives, going down
To their busy market-town,
Hear me wheedling: "Lady, please,
Pretty lady, buy a cheese!"
And I never find it matters
That I'm nicknamed Rags-and-Tatters,
For they buy my fairy cheeses,
Freshest, finest, fairy cheeses!

M

Nasturtium

◆ THE SONG OF ◆
THE NASTURTIUM FAIRY

Nasturtium the jolly,
　　O ho, O ho!
He holds up his brolly
　　Just so, just so!
(A shelter from showers,
　　A shade from the sun;)
’Mid flame-coloured flowers
　　He grins at the fun.
Up fences he scrambles,
　　Sing hey, sing hey!
All summer he rambles
　　So gay, so gay—
Till the night-frost strikes chilly,
　　And Autumn leaves fall,
And he’s gone, willy-nilly,
　　Umbrella and all.

Orchis

◆ THE SONG OF ◆
THE ORCHIS FAIRY

The families of orchids,
    they are the strangest clan,
With spots and twists resembling
    a bee, or fly, or man;
And some are in the hot-house,
    and some in foreign lands,
But Early Purple Orchis
    in English pasture stands.

He loves the grassy hill-top,
    he breathes the April air;
He knows the baby rabbits,
    he knows the Easter hare,
The nesting of the skylarks,
    the bleat of lambkins too,
The cowslips, and the rainbow,
    the sunshine, and the dew.

O orchids of the hot-house,
    what miles away you are!
O flaming tropic orchids,
    how far, how very far!

Pansy

◆ THE SONG OF ◆
THE PANSY FAIRY

Pansy and Petunia,
Periwinkle, Pink—
How to choose the best of them,
Leaving out the rest of them,
That is hard, I think.

Poppy with its pepper-pots,
Polyanthus, Pea—
Though I wouldn't slight the rest,
Isn't Pansy *quite* the best,
Quite the best for P?

Black and brown and velvety,
Purple, yellow, red;
Loved by people big and small,
All who plant and dig at all
In a garden bed.

Queen of the Meadow

◆ THE SONG OF THE ◆
QUEEN OF THE MEADOW FAIRY

Queen of the Meadow
  where small streams are flowing,
What is your kingdom
  and whom do you rule?
"Mine are the places
  where wet grass is growing,
Mine are the people
  of marshland and pool.

"Kingfisher-courtiers,
  swift-flashing, beautiful,
Dragon-flies, minnows,
  are mine one and all;
Little frog-servants who
  wait round me, dutiful,
Hop on my errands
  and come when I call."

Gentle Queen Meadowsweet,
  served with such loyalty,
Have you no crown then,
  no jewels to wear?
"Nothing I need
  for a sign of my royalty,
Nothing at all
  but my own fluffy hair!"

Ragged   Robin

◆ THE SONG OF ◆
THE RAGGED ROBIN FAIRY

In wet marshy meadows
A tattered piper strays—
Ragged, ragged Robin;
On thin reeds he plays.

He asks for no payment;
He plays, for delight,
A tune for the fairies
To dance to, at night.

They nod and they whisper,
And say, looking wise,
"A princeling is Robin,
For all his disguise!"

◆ THE SONG OF ◆
THE STRAWBERRY FAIRY

A flower for S!
Is Sunflower he?
He's handsome, yes,
But what of me?—

In my party suit
Of red and white,
And a gift of fruit
For the feast tonight:

Strawberries small
And wild and sweet,
For the Queen and all
Of her Court to eat!

Thrift

◆ THE SONG OF ◆
THE THRIFT FAIRY

Now will we tell of splendid things:
Seagulls, that sail on fearless wings
Where great cliffs tower, grand and high
Against the blue, blue summer sky.
Where none but birds (and sprites) can go.
Oh there the rosy sea-pinks grow,
(Sea-pinks, whose other name is Thrift);
They fill each crevice, chink, and rift
Where no one climbs; and at the top,
Too near the edge for sheep to crop,
Thick in the grass pink patches show.
The sea lies sparkling far below.
Oh lucky Thrift, to live so free
Between blue sky and bluer sea!

◆ THE SONG OF ◆
THE VETCH FAIRY

Poor little U
Has nothing to do!
He hasn't a flower: not one.
For U is Unlucky, I'm sorry to tell;
U stands for Unfortunate, Ugly as well;
No single sweet flowery name will it spell—
Is there nothing at all to be done?
"Don't fret, little neighbour,"
    says kind fairy V,
"You're welcome to share
    all my flowers with me—
Come, play with them, laugh, and have fun.
I've Vetches in plenty for me and for you,
Verbena, Valerian, Violets too:
Don't cry then, because you have none."

Vetch

(There are many kinds of Vetch; some are in
the hay-fields, but this is Tufted Vetch, which
climbs in the hedges.)

153

Wallflower

◆ THE SONG OF ◆
THE WALLFLOWER FAIRY

Wallflower, Wallflower, up on the wall,
Who sowed your seed there?
                    "No one at all:
Long, long ago it was blown by the breeze
To the crannies of walls
    where I live as I please.

"Garden walls, castle walls, mossy and old,
These are my dwellings;
    from these I behold
The changes of years;
    yet, each spring that goes by,
Unchanged in my sweet-smelling
    velvet am I!"

Yellow Deadnettle

◆ THE SONG OF ◆
THE YELLOW DEADNETTLE FAIRY

You saucy X! You love to vex
Your next-door neighbour Y:
And just because no flower is yours,
You tease him on the sly.
Straight, yellow, tall,—of Nettles all,
The handsomest is his;
He thinks no ill, and wonders still
What all your mischief is.
Yet have a care! Bad imp, beware
His upraised hand and arm:
Though stingless, he comes leaping—see!—
To save his flower from harm.

Zinnia

◆ THE SONG OF ◆
THE ZINNIA FAIRY

Z for Zinnias, pink or red;
See them in the flower-bed,
Copper, orange, all aglow,
Making such a stately show.

I, their fairy, say Good-bye,
For the last of all am I.
Now the Alphabet is said
All the way from A to Z.

OLD RHYMES
for all
TIMES

◆

◆ A FAIRY WENT A-MARKETING ◆

A fairy went a-marketing –
   She bought a little fish;
She put it in a crystal bowl
   Upon a golden dish.
An hour she sat in wonderment
   And watched its silver gleam,
And then she gently took it up
   And slipped it in a stream.

A fairy went a-marketing –
   She bought a coloured bird;
It sang the sweetest, shrillest song
   That ever she had heard.
She sat beside its painted cage
   And listened half the day,
And then she opened wide the door
   And let it fly away.

A fairy went a-marketing –
   She bought a winter gown
All stitched about with gossamer
   And lined with thistledown.
She wore it all the afternoon
   With prancing and delight,
Then gave it to a little frog
   To keep him warm at night.

A fairy went a-marketing –
   She bought a gentle mouse
To take her tiny messages,
   To keep her tiny house.
All day she kept its busy feet
   Pit-patting to and fro,
And then she kissed its silken ears,
   Thanked it, and let it go.

Rose Fyleman

◆ BERRIES ◆

There was an old woman
    Went blackberry picking
Along the hedges
    From Weep to Wicking.
Half a pottle –
    No more had she got,
When out steps a Fairy
    From her green grot;
And says, "Well, Jill,
    Would 'ee pick 'ee mo?"
And Jill, she curtseys,
    And looks just so.
"Be off," says the Fairy,
    "As quick as you can,
Over the meadows
    To the little green lane,
That dips to the hayfields
    Of Farmer Grimes:
I've berried those hedges
    A score of times;

Bushel on bushel
        I'll promise 'ee, Jill,
This side of supper
        If 'ee pick with a will."
She glints very bright,
        And speaks her fair;
Then lo, and behold!
        She had faded in air.

Be sure Old Goodie
        She trots betimes
Over the meadows
        To Farmer Grimes.
And never was queen
        With jewellery rich
As those same hedges
        From twig to ditch;
Like Dutchman's coffers,
        Fruit, thorn, and flower –
They shone like William
        And Mary's bower.
And be sure Old Goodie
        Went back to Weep,
So tired with her basket
        She scarce could creep.

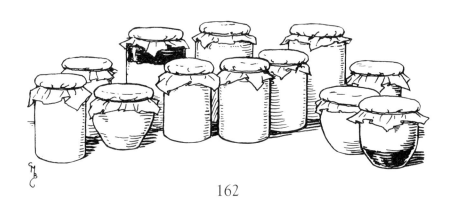

When she comes in the dusk
     To her cottage door,
There's Towser wagging
     As never before,
To see his Missus
     So glad to be
Come from her fruit-picking
     Back to he.

As soon as next morning
     Dawn was grey,
The pot on the hob
     Was simmering away;
And all in a stew
     And a hugger-mugger
Towser and Jill
     A-boiling of sugar,
And the dark clear fruit
     That from Faërie came,
For syrup and jelly
     And blackberry jam.

Twelve jolly gallipots
     Jill put by;
And one little teeny one,
     One inch high;
And that she's hidden
     A good thumb deep,
Halfway over
     From Wicking to Weep.

Walter de la Mare

◆ THE FAIRIES ◆

If ye will with Mab find grace,
Set each Platter in his place:
Rake the Fire up, and get
Water in; ere Sun be set.
Wash your Pails, and cleanse your Dairies;
Sluts are loathsome to the Fairies:
Sweep your house: Who doth not so,
Mab will pinch her by the toe.

Robert Herrick

◆ THE FAERIE FAIR ◆

The fairies hold a fair, they say,
Beyond the hills when skies are grey
And daylight things are laid away.

And very strange their marketing,
If we could see them on the wing
With all the fairy ware they bring.

Long strings they sell, of berries bright,
And wet wind-fallen apples light
Blown from the trees some starry night.

Gay patches, too, for tattered wings,
Gold bubbles blown by goblin things,
And mushrooms for the fairy rings.

Fine flutes are there, of magic reed,
Whose piping sets the elves indeed
A-dancing down the dewy mead.

These barter they for bats and moles,
For beaten silver bells and bowls,
Bright from the caverns of the Trolls.

And so they show, and sell and buy,
With song and dance right merrily,
Until the morning gilds the sky.

Florence Harrison

The Fairy
Necklaces

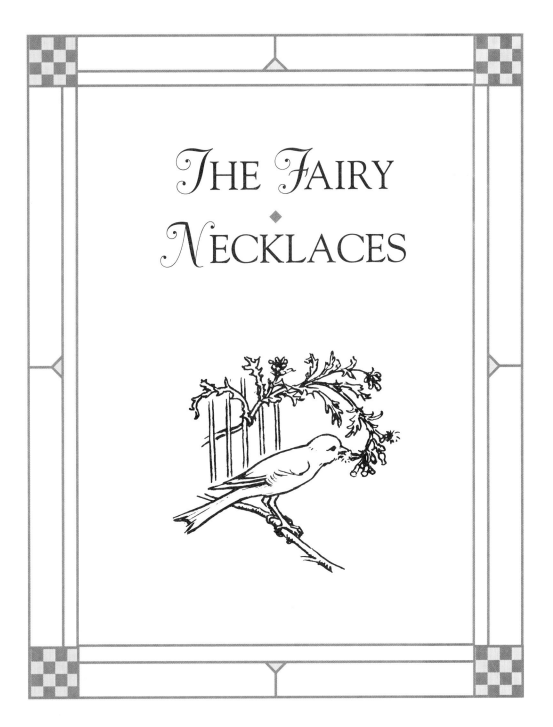

A JOB FOR JENNY

◆

Once upon a time, in the days when more fairies were about than now, a little girl named Jenny Wilkie was sitting outside the back-door of a cottage, in a hollow called Frog's Hole. It was an old thatched cottage, with an untidy garden, and one apple-tree covered with pink blossom; and pleasant fields sloped around it.

Jenny was sewing busily; her stiches were, perhaps, not *very* small and neat — she was making a bonnet for her doll, and was in a hurry to try it on. Just then, out of the door hobbled a grumpy-looking old man. He gave a poke with his stick at the odds and ends and dolls' clothes which lay beside Jenny, and said:

"Can't you find something better to do, than waste your time with this rubbish?"

Jenny looked up at him.

"Claribell needs a new bonnet very badly," said she. "But still — *is* there something else you would like me to do, Great-Uncle?"

"Any amount of things a handy boy or girl would do, and that I'd do myself if it weren't for my rheumatics. But that lazy loon Robin never shows himself except at meals, and you just idle away your time when you're not at school. I've no patience to see the place going to wrack and ruin, and you two youngsters never giving it a thought."

"Poor Great-Uncle! I wish your rheumatics weren't so bad," said Jenny. She laid down the bonnet. "*What* would you like me to do?" she asked again.

Great-Uncle Jeremiah looked around.

"You might weed the cabbage-patch, if you

could be trusted to pull up the groundsel and leave the cabbages," he said.

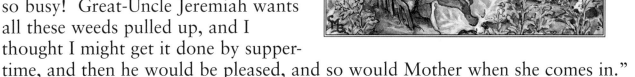

"Why yes, Great-Uncle; I'll do it, ever so carefully!" said Jenny, jumping up.

She took a garden fork, and set to work. Great-Uncle Jeremiah watched for a few minutes, then hobbled back into the cottage.

Jenny had not been working long, when the freckled face of a boy, older than herself, appeared over the broken fence. He called out:

"Jenny! Come here! Come and see what I've made!"

"Oh Robin!" she answered, "I'm so busy! Great-Uncle Jeremiah wants all these weeds pulled up, and I thought I might get it done by supper-time, and then he would be pleased, and so would Mother when she comes in."

"Why, isn't she in yet?" said Robin.

"No; don't you remember, she said they would be spring-cleaning at the Great House, and she would be late?"

"I didn't notice," said Robin. Then he said:

"When I'm a man, I'll make lots of money, and mother shan't ever go out to work for the Miss Hoopcocks or anyone else!"

"*How* will you make lots of money?" inquired Jenny, with interest.

"I'll be an inventor, and invent a new kind of water-mill or windmill, or something. Jenny, *do* come. I've made a little water-wheel and it's turning just like a real one, down at the brook. You *must* look!"

"Well, just for a minute," said Jenny. She slipped through a gap in the fence, and they ran together to the little stream which flowed at the bottom of Frog's Hole, where Robin showed the clever toy he had made, and Jenny was full of admiration.

JENNY'S PLAN

◆

Jenny soon came back, wriggled through the fence, and went on weeding; and as she weeded she was thinking harder than she had ever done before.

She thought of her mother, coming home so late and tired from work.

The Wilkies had lived with Great-Uncle Jeremiah ever since Jenny's father died, too long ago for her to remember; and Mrs. Wilkie scrubbed and washed and ironed to earn money to feed and clothe them all.

"Robin is always thinking what he will do when he is grown-up; how can I earn some money for Mother, *now*?" thought Jenny.

Suddenly she stopped and looked at the pile of groundsel she had pulled up. Didn't people give groundsel to canaries? And there couldn't be much of it in towns.

If she tied it in bunches, and took it to market, she might sell it, and bring the money home to Mother.

Market-day was Saturday, when there was no school, and she did errands for her mother in the town; and tomorrow *was* Saturday.

So, instead of throwing all the weeds on the rubbish-heap, Jenny fetched some water from the spring, put the groundsel into it to keep fresh, and hid it behind some bushes. She had no time to make up the bunches then, for Mother had come home, and was calling her to supper; and, oh dear, what a mess she was in, with her pinafore wet and dirty, and her hands all covered in mud! And she had not finished the weeding, nor Claribell's bonnet, nor tidied away her things; and I fear she was scolded, for that was Great-Uncle's way, and even Mother was a little bit cross.

But Jenny did not take much heed; she sat quietly eating her bread and milk, and planning just what she would do next day.

"The ladies want me tomorrow morning," said Mrs. Wilkie, during supper. "I'll make a list tonight of the things you're to get in town, Jenny. They'll be a bit heavy, I'm afraid; Robin might have gone with you to carry them, only I need him to fetch some flour from the mill. Robin, do you hear?"

For, with Robin, things often "went in at one ear and out at the other"; but he had heard, this time, and nodded. An errand to the mill was what he liked.

Jenny was pleased, too, because she wanted to keep her plan a secret.

She woke early next morning, and crept out of bed, moving as quietly as she could, so as not to wake her mother, in whose room she slept. But Mrs. Wilkie's eyes did open, and looked with surprise at Jenny, half-dressed.

"I'm going in the garden. I may, Mother, mayn't I?" asked Jenny.

"If you like, dear; but don't get tired before your long walk! I must be stirring soon, myself," replied Mrs. Wilkie.

So Jenny ran out into the dewy garden. She cut the earthy roots off the groundsel, tied it in bunches, arranged it in a basket, and covered it over with a duster. Then she went a little way up the lane, just out of sight of the cottage, hid the basket by the stile, ran back, and finished weeding the cabbage-patch.

Mrs. Wilkie, meanwhile, was stirring indeed: lighting the fire, shaking the mats, sweeping the kitchen, cooking the porridge, and sending Robin to pump the water and fetch the milk from the farm.

After breakfast she gave Jenny the money and shopping-list.

"Take a basket," said Mrs.Wilkie, "and start soon. I shall be home to see about dinner; mind you aren't late!"

She hurried off, down the path that led to the plank bridge over the stream, and through a little wood, to the Great House.

Great-Uncle Jeremiah stood at the door to see Jenny start. He watched her go, running and swinging the empty basket. "You'll lose the money if you aren't careful!" he called after her.

He would have been surprised if he had seen her, round the bend of the lane, bring out a second basket from its hiding-place, peep under the duster which covered it, and go on her way with a basket on each arm and a very busy look on her face.

MR PETERCOO

◆

It was a long way, all uphill; but Jenny was lucky — she was given a lift in one of the farm carts, and reached the market early.

She did her mother's errands first; then put the basket of marketings behind the stall of a woman who knew her, and started on her new adventure.

But though she stood very patiently at a corner of the Market Square with her groundsel, she sold very few bunches. The passers-by seemed too busy to take any notice of her.

Perhaps, she thought, if she went into the side streets, she would do better; people might be less busy there.

After a time she happened to stand still in front of a little shop, over the window of which was painted "W. PETERCOO, Watch-maker and Jeweller". She was looking sadly at her groundsel, which, as groundsel quickly does, had become quite limp in the hot sunshine, when the door opened, and an old man with a kind thin face looked out.

"Are you selling that groundsel, little girl?" he asked.

"Yes, sir, I *was*; a penny a bunch; but I'm afraid it's not much good now!" replied Jenny.

"It will freshen up in water; I'll take six penn'orth!" said the old man. Jenny's face showed her delight.

"Have you a great many canaries, sir?" she asked.

"I have; and I can't often get out to find groundsel for them. I should be glad of a groundsel-merchant to come to my door!"

"Do you mean me, sir?" said Jenny.

"That is what I mean; I'll buy again, if you come another day. Where do you live?"

"At Frog's Hole, sir."

"Frog's Hole? It sounds a damp spot."

"It is, sir. Mother thinks that's why Great-Uncle Jeremiah has such rheumatics."

"Dear, dear! And where *is* Frog's Hole?"

"Just beyond Willow farm."

"A long way!" Mr Petercoo seemed to be considering Jenny, looking at her so kindly that she ventured to ask him for a drink.

"Certainly, certainly!" he said; and he took her into the shop and brought her a glass of water. While she drank it, he asked her how she meant to spend her money.

"I'm not going to spend it; I want it for Mother, so she need not work so hard," explained Jenny.

"And how much have you got?" inquired Mr. Petercoo.

"Elevenpence, with what you gave me," she replied showing him the money.

"H'm!" said the old gentleman. "Well, I advise you to save it, till you have earned a bit more; you can count on me as a regular customer. Don't forget — Mr. Petercoo, Watchmaker and Jeweller!"

Jenny thanked him, and went away much cheered.

Next saturday, she found Mr. Petercoo's shop again; she had some beautiful fresh groundsel for him and again he bought six bunches. A mug of milk and a piece of gingerbread were waiting for her, and this time he showed her his canaries. They were in a big open-air cage, or aviary, built out from the room at the back of the shop; it took up nearly all the tiny garden. Some of the canaries were flying about, some singing on perches, and Mr. Petercoo knew them all apart. Some were so tame, they would sit on his finger, and take a seed from between his lips.

Jenny would have liked to stay and watch them, but the shop bell rang, Mr. Petercoo hurried to serve a customer, and Jenny had to go.

But she and Mr. Petercoo soon became great friends.

If she had been more with her mother, Jenny could hardly have kept the secret; she nearly said, "Mr. Petercoo told me this or that," once or twice, as it was. But not quite.

Each Saturday, when she brought the groundsel, he paid with a silver sixpence, and let her stay for a while to look at the canaries, or admire the jewellery in his glass cases, or see him take a watch to pieces in the little room behind the shop.

Not many customers came; for though Mr. Petercoo mended clocks and watches cleverly, and knew all about precious stones, people seldom bought anything, or even looked in the window, because he was too poor to be able to keep his shop stocked with new and fashionable goods. But he lived very contentedly with his canaries.

Jenny and he talked of what they would do if they were rich. Jenny chose which of his best brooches she would buy as a present for Mrs. Wilkie; while Mr. Petercoo's idea was to put a drinking-fountain in the Square for thirsty children, and a seat, where the evening sun caught the church wall, "for the old fellows like me to sit on, after shop-hours," he said.

"I suppose one would have to be *very* rich to do those things," Jenny said, thoughtfully.

"I've only got four-and-sevenpence yet, for Mother. Shall I give it to her, do you think, when it is five shillings?"

"I think she would consider that a very useful sum of money," said Mr. Petercoo.

A WISH

◆

A few days after this, Jenny came running home from school to get ready to go to her friend Marigold's birthday party. Claribell was invited too; she sat waiting on Jenny's bed, in a gay new dress made by Mrs. Wilkie out of bits of silk from the Great House.

Jenny loved to go across the fields to Willow Farm. The farmer and his wife were kind and jolly, there was plenty of everything nice, and there was Marigold's curly-haired baby sister to play with. As Jenny washed her face and hands, and brushed her hair, she thought to herself how lucky Marigold was.

"But I shall see her presents," thought Jenny, "and I shall have some of her birthday cake; so I'm lucky too. I haven't got a party dress, but I'll put on my necklace."

She opened her drawer, and took out a string of glass beads, of mixed colours, which she had threaded herself; she always wore them on special occasions, because she had no other pretty thing to wear. As she looked at them, a tiny voice outside the window began to sing, in a wheedling kind of way; *such* a tiny voice, that Jenny thought it must be a little bird's — and yet, surely, she heard her own name?

"Jenny Wilkie, Jenny Wilkie,
If your clothes were fine and silky,
Decked with necklaces and brooches,
And you drove about in coaches;
If your purse were stuffed with money;
If your bread were thick with honey,
And your porridge sweet and milky -
Jenny Wilkie, Jenny Wilkie,
What a happy girl you'd be!"

Jenny put her head out of the window and looked around; but no, she could see nothing unusual. While she wondered, another little voice, sweeter than the first, but with an anxious sound in it, began to sing:

"Jenny darling, Jenny darling,
Listen to the whistling starling;
To the creatures bleating, mooing,
Quacking, grunting, cackling, cooing;
To the farmyard cock a-crowing,
Or the rippling stream a-flowing;
Never listen, darling Jenny,
(Though his words are soft as any),
To that singer in the tree!"

"Well I never" thought Jenny, "But I *still* can't see anything or anybody! Can it have been my fancy? Whatever it was, I musn't be late for the party!"
She took up her beads again.
"Claribell!" she said suddenly, "wouldn't it be nice to choose which necklace to put on, instead of only having one! *I wish I had a different one for every day in the year!*"

Then she laughed. "Oh no, that's silly! There are 365 days in the year — I learnt that at school today — and 365 necklaces would be too many. Mine's very nice; and you look lovely, Claribell! We're ready now; come along!"

She picked up her doll and ran downstairs.

* * * * * * * *

An Elf and a Fairy, hidden in the apple-tree close to Jenny's window, sat and looked at one another.

"Why did you interfere with my song?" asked the Elf.

"Because it was mean to try to make that human child discontented, when she has so few nice things," replied the Fairy.

"Well," said the Elf "you heard her wish? Let's be friends, and give it her! She'll have nice things then — lots of them!"

"I don't quite trust you," said the Fairy; "You know you're full of mischief! But it would be a grand surprise for Jenny. If she were proud, or greedy, or stupid, such a gift would only bring squabbles and misfortune; but I really believe she is sweet-natured enough for it to bring good luck, and not bad."

"Now I come to think of it," remarked the Elf, "where can we get all those necklaces? She said 365!"

The Fairy knew what to do.

They would go to the Fairy Queen, she said; tell her about the wish, and, if she approved, take an order signed by her to the Trolls, the fairy jewellers, who live in the mountain caverns.

Other fairies would go with them, to help carry the necklaces. But the Elf must promise to be a Good Elf, and not play tricks any more.

He promised.

"Come then," cried the Fairy; "if we lose no time, we'll be back here by midnight!"

There was a flutter, and they were gone.

THE FAIRY GIFT

◆

Just after midnight, Jenny turned over in her bed, and opened her eyes. What had wakened her? Had she been dreaming? Or had she really seen a cloud of big butterflies, of all the prettiest colours, flying out of the open window as she awoke?

It must have been a dream. There was the quiet room, just as usual, Mother asleep in the other bed, and the calm bright moon looking in.

And yet — Jenny felt sure something *had* moved; something *had* happened. She sat up, crept to the foot of the bed, meaning to look out of the window, and saw — what?

On the floor, in the moonlight, stood a large box, or chest. It had silvery handles at the sides, it shone with inlaid mother-o'-pearl, and a silver key was in its lock.

Jenny gazed, spellbound; then she slipped down from her bed to look more closely. As she looked, her eyes grew bigger and rounder; and she called out: "Mammie, Mammie, wake up! Wake up! Oh, come and look!"

Mrs. Wilkie woke at once, and sprang out of bed asking what was the matter.

"Oh Mammie, a present from the fairies!" cried Jenny, pointing to a label which was tied to one of the handles of the chest. She had read it by the bright moonlight, but Mrs. Wilkie lit a candle to see better. *"To Jenny Wilkie, a Present from the Fairies."* And, to make quite certain whose the box was, there were the letters J.W. in silver on the lid.

You can fancy Mrs. Wilkie's exclamations of surprise; and when Jenny turned the key and lifted the lid, they both gave such shrieks of astonishment that Great-Uncle Jeremiah heard, and came hurrying in, in his night-shirt and nightcap. For the box was full of nothing but necklaces, dozens and dozens of them, of every kind, lying on velvet-covered trays. As Jenny, half dazed, lifted up each tray, there were more necklaces beneath — coral, turquoise, amber, and pearls; opals, amethysts, and moonstones; beads of ivory, strings of tiny shells, chains of silver and chains of gold — more varied and more lovely than all Mr. Petercoo's stock put together.

"Are we all dreaming?" asked Mrs. Wilkie.

Jenny, who had a feeling that the necklaces might vanish as mysteriously as they had come, rushed to Robin's little room, woke him, and dragged him in to see them too. He stared open-mouthed; then squatted down and began quietly counting the necklaces.

"But are they *real*? I hardly dare touch them, myself!" said Mrs. Wilkie. "If they *are* real, our fortune is made! Oh, my little Jenny, why should the fairies have given such a gift to *you*?"

Before she could answer, Great-Uncle Jeremiah, who seemed to have been struck dumb until then, suddenly found his voice.

"What I say is this," he pronounced, "all my life I have heard tales of fairy gifts, and there's always a catch in them somewhere. Don't you be too set up till you see those necklaces by daylight. Depend upon it, they're all moonshine, to make a mock of us; and when you look for them tomorrow, you'll find nothing but worthless pebbles and dust. *I* shall go back to bed, and advise you all to do the same. There's Jenny — she'll catch her death of cold; and then what good will necklaces be to her?"

So saying, he went off, and slammed his bedroom door. Mrs. Wilkie wrapped a blanket round Jenny, who was shivering, but more from excitement than cold; and Robin looked up from his counting.

"I think there are 365!" he said.

Jenny flushed crimson.

"Why," she said, "that is what I wished for — one for every day in the year! But I didn't really mean it!"

"You wished for them?" said Mrs. Wilkie.

"Whatever made you do that? Did you *see* a fairy?"

"Oh, no, I never saw any fairy, though I did hear some funny little voices calling my name. I was getting ready for Marigold's party, and putting on my necklace; and I just said to Claribell, that I wished I had a different one for every day in the year. I never thought any more about it — but they've come!"

"Well," said Mrs. Wilkie, "it's past my understanding. I suppose we must just do as your Great-Uncle said: go back to bed, and wait for the morning."

But there was not much sleep at Frog's Hole that night!

WHAT NEXT?

◆

Next morning, the necklaces were still there; and very early Jenny was trying them on, one after another, in front of the glass.

Great-Uncle Jeremiah, in spite of what he had said, was eager as Jenny herself to see them by the light of day; and when he found that they were quite real, and even more beautiful than they had seemed by candlelight, a surprising thing happened — he slapped his knees and burst into a fit of cackling laughter.

At the sight of his old face, wrinkled into such unaccustomed lines, the others began laughing too, until Mrs. Wilkie looked quite pink and young. Robin, shouting "Three cheers for Jenny!" caught and hugged her as she went dancing about the room.

Great-Uncle Jeremiah collapsed into a chair, wiping his eyes.

"Bravo! Bravo!" he said; "come and give your old Great-Uncle a kiss, Jenny!"

He had never said such a thing before; but Jenny, forgetful of past scoldings, ran to him and threw her arms round his neck, while Mrs. Wilkie looked on in astonishment. She thought of frozen water, thawing: the ice had cracked, and, surely, was melting away in the sunshine!

At breakfast he and Mrs. Wilkie sobered down, and began to discuss what was to be done with the necklaces.

"If it gets known that they are here, we shall have thieves, without a doubt," said the old man. "The children must understand, they are not to breathe a word to anybody. I wish I knew some trustworthy person, who understands such things, to tell us what the necklaces are worth, and how best to sell them; for that's the only sensible thing to do."

Jenny, listening, thought to herself: "He's forgotten that there's one for every day in the year; I'm sure the fairies meant me to wear them!" But she did not like to say so.

"They are certainly not safe here," agreed Mrs. Wilkie; "but after all, they are Jenny's, so oughtn't they be kept for her somewhere until she is grown up? What a dowry for her when she marries!"

"Mayn't I have just a few, to wear now, and give to people?" Jenny ventured to ask.

"We'll see, darling," replied Mrs. Wilkie; "we must think it all over. You and Robin must go to school as usual, but not say a word about the necklaces; I must go to the Great House, and Great-Uncle will mind the box; and we'll try and think who can advise us."

Jenny plucked up her courage.

"Mother," she said, "there's Mr. Petercoo in the town. He's a jeweller, and very kind; I think he would help."

A great deal of questioning and explanation followed.

Jenny had to tell the whole story of her groundsel selling; and she brought out her little hoard of pennies and sixpences, which was so nearly five shillings, and gave it to her mother, who, being bewildered already, hardly knew whether to praise or blame Jenny for what she had done. And meanwhile, Great-Uncle Jeremiah was repeating: "Petercoo! Petercoo! I knew a William Petercoo when we were both lads. If this is the same, he's a good fellow; but I didn't know he was back in these parts."

Robin and Jenny were late for school that morning. Robin was caned for inattention and Jenny fell asleep over her sums; and the teacher, who could not make her out, told her she had better go to bed instead of coming back in the afternoon. It was hard to keep the secret at playtime; Jenny couldn't help whispering to Marigold that "something wonderful had happened — she mustn't say what!"

The two rushed home at dinner-time, and found that Mrs. Wilkie had decided to go to see Mr. Petercoo; she had asked to be spared from the Great House as she had "unexpected business in the town".

Great-Uncle Jeremiah, who had spent the morning pondering over the necklaces, was more anxious than ever to get them out of the cottage before nightfall, for fear of robbers; "and yet," he said, "the jewels may be shams, and worthless after all. I shall go with you to Petercoo, and we'll take the whole lot along with us, and find out the truth."

"Oh, but, Uncle," said Mrs. Wilkie, "you can never walk so far! You haven't been to town for years!"

"I can if I take my time," said Great-Uncle Jeremiah.

MR PETERCOO'S ADVICE

◆

An odd little party arrived at Mr. Petercoo's shop late that afternoon: Great-Uncle, in a tall chimney-pot hat, which Jenny had never seen him wear before; Jenny herself, in a state of mixed excitement and shyness; Mrs. Wilkie in her best shawl and bonnet; and Robin pushing a wheel-barrow in which was a mysterious package wrapped in sacks.

The two old men recognized each other with delight.

" 'Pon my word, William Petercoo, after all these years!"

"Bless my soul, if it's not Jeremiah Titmuss! And I never guessed that was who the little maid meant, when she talked about her Great-Uncle!"

Jenny thought the hand-shaking would never stop; but at last they were all gathered in the little room behind the shop, and Mr. Petercoo began to understand why they had come. When the chest was opened, he lifted out tray after tray with trembling fingers.

"I've always heard that the Little People are wonderful jewellers," he said;

"I'd give something to see the tools that cut and polished these stones, and the little hammers that forged this gold and silver!"

"Then they *are* of value?" said Mrs. Wilkie.

"Undoubtedly! though not equally so. It will take time to go through them carefully. Some are merely pretty trifles; but some — "

He paused, and looked lovingly at a beautiful string of pearls; then took up a necklace shimmering with the colours of the sea.

"*Some*," he continued, "are the most exquisite things I have ever handled. This, now — aquamarines and emeralds, with little pearls between! This is fit for the highest in the land to wear! And as for these diamonds — "

He paused again, taking up a sparkling necklet, with a pendant of one glorious sapphire surrounded with tiny diamonds.

" — *These* are probably worth all the rest put together!"

"And they are all *mine*?" said Jenny softly, going close to Mr. Petercoo; "they really belong to *me*?"

"Why yes," he answered; "and we must put on our thinking-caps to help you to do wisely with them. Not even the Queen could wear so many necklaces; certainly not a little lass like you. You wanted to help your dear mother" ("she did indeed, Ma'am," he said to Mrs. Wilkie) "and now you'll be able to do far more than you ever dreamed! Isn't that a fine thing, Jenny?"

"Yes," she answered; but in such a doubtful voice that Mr. Petercoo, said encouragingly, "What is it, my dear? Don't be afraid to speak out!"

"Do you think that fairies will *mind*? Is it polite to sell their presents?" asked Jenny.

Mr. Petercoo, Great-Uncle Jeremiah, and Mrs. Wilkie all looked at one another rather blankly. None of them had thought of that.

Then Mrs. Wilkie said: "Surely, if *good* fairies were the givers, they can only wish to see Jenny happy and prosperous; and if *bad* fairies —"

"If *bad* fairies," put in Great-Uncle Jeremiah, with a touch of his old manner, "the gift will bring ill-luck whatever we do."

"From what I've heard," said Mr. Petercoo, thoughtfully, 'the things that displease the fairies are greediness and ingratitude. They don't like their gifts to be snatched at, and hoarded selfishly. No! If Jenny shows her pleasure always wearing one or other of the necklaces (suitable ones, of course) and gives some away to her friends, I think we may safely sell the rest. And I think, my dear," he said to Jenny, "before you get into bed tonight, you should stand at your open window and say: "Thank you, kind fairies, for your beautiful present!"

He put a string of coral beads round her neck, then and there; and after further talk it was agreed that he should take charge of all the other necklaces, sort out some for Jenny to wear or give away, and lock the rest in the big safe in his cellar to be sold by degrees.

Jenny understood that part of the money would be saved for her until she was grown-up, and part would be used straightaway by Mrs. Wilkie.

"You must take a share for yourself, Petercoo: that's business," said Great-Uncle Jeremiah.

Mr Petercoo thanked him, but thought not. It would be a pleasure to sell them, he said, and would bring new customers to the shop.

On the way home, Great-Uncle Jeremiah remarked: "That's a snug little place of Petercoo's! And the air is fresh in the town there, standing high as it does. Very different from Frog's Hole!"

MORE ABOUT NECKLACES

◆

Mr. Petercoo feared there was no one in the little market-town rich enough to buy the diamond necklace. This troubled him, and he wondered whether he ought to take it to London to sell, shutting his shop for a week.

However, that must wait — there were plenty of others to deal with!

He let Jenny choose a lovely gold chain and locket for her mother, and the next Saturday afternoon the little girl gathered her schoolmates in the meadow, to share the necklaces which Mr. Petercoo had picked out for her to do as she liked with.

They sat round, pretending to be Princesses and Duchesses: Kitty, Rosie, Meg, Molly and Liz with blue, pink, yellow, green, and red beads; Mary with a silver chain and locket; Dorothy, tiny many-coloured shells, and Sally, purple and green ones. Marigold had little ivory daisies with yellow middles; and her baby sister had pretty bead forget-me-nots.

Jenny kept for herself some beads which held all the lovely colours of soap-bubbles.

One necklace took Robin's fancy — a curious foreign-looking thing. Its gay beads were of odd sizes and colours; in front was a worn silver coin (from what land, he could not make out) and, for fastening, a leather loop went over a big red bead. Jenny gave it to him, and he hung it on a nail in his room, and liked to look at it and wonder — had the fairies stolen it from the pack of some pedlar? Had it been washed up on the seashore, from some wreck? Or was it part of some buried treasure, forgotten long ago? Who could tell?

Tales of Jenny's good fortune soon went about; though nobody knew, at first, that it had anything to do with the change in Mr. Petercoo's shop, away in the town, where people now crowded to look in the window, and business was so brisk that he began to think of taking an assistant.

One day the grand Miss Hoopcocks drove out in their carriage, and rustled into the shop, nearly filling it with their stiff silk dresses.

They bought several necklaces. Mr. Petercoo chuckled to himself when they chose two which, he knew, Jenny did not think very pretty — one of agate and one of carnelian; and when they departed, as he bowed politely, there was a twinkle in his eye, for he knew who they were. What would they have said, he wondered, had they known that the necklaces came from their charwoman's little girl?

Soon, they did know; for with money coming in, Mrs. Wilkie found she need not go out to work any more, and told them the whole story.

Then began happy days at Frog's Hole.

Sitting under the apple-tree with her sewing, Mrs. Wilkie told Jenny of her hopes.

"Robin will be leaving school next year," she said "I never thought I should be able to apprentice him (that means, pay for him to learn a proper trade). But with your money, Jenny, I think I can."

"Can he be a blacksmith, or a miller?" asked Jenny, who knew Robin's wishes.

Mrs. Wilkie thought he could.

"And if we could get out of this damp, tumbledown cottage," she continued, "I'm sure your Great-Uncle would be better."

MISS SELINA HOOP-COCK

MISS BELINDA HOOP-COCK

"There's a little house called Tickletakes, the other side of the farm, that I've always liked. I hear the people are leaving it, but I don't know whether we could afford it, or Uncle Jeremiah would go there. We must wait and see."

Jenny went to look at Tickletakes. How pleasant it looked, with its sweet-briar hedge, its garden full of pinks and lavender and roses, its fruit-trees, and everything, she thought, that one could wish!

MR. PETERCOO'S TRIUMPH

◆

Jenny did not forget Mr. Petercoo's canaries, but still took them a bunch of groundsel each Saturday, as a present; and stayed in the shop, seeing which necklaces were on view, and learning the names of the precious stones, until Mrs. Wilkie (who did her own marketing now) came to fetch her.

Then, one evening, Mr. Petercoo came walking out to Frog's Hole with great news.

He had sold the diamond necklace!

A Prince, he said, had heard of the wonderful necklaces, and came to the town, inquiring for the shop where they were sold. He was seeking the

loveliest birthday present he could buy for the Princess he was going to marry.

He examined some necklaces, and then asked: "Are these the very best you have?"

This was Mr. Petercoo's chance. He hurried down to the cellar, unlocked the safe, and brought out the diamonds.

Directly the Prince saw them, with their glorious sapphire he knew he

had found the present worthy of his Princess, and willingly paid the price of £1000.

Before he left the shop, he said; "I hear there is a remarkable story about these necklaces; I should like to know it, to tell the Princess." So Mr. Petercoo told him all about Jenny.

What excitement there was at Frog's Hole!

"*Dear* Mr. Petercoo!" cried Jenny, hugging him; "it is all your doing!"

"Indeed, indeed," said Mrs. Wilkie, "we can never thank you enough for your help!"

"But how could I have helped at all," asked Mr. Petercoo, "if Jenny had never come groundsel-selling to my door? It is all *her* doing, it seems to me!"

✤ ✤ ✤ ✤ ✤ ✤ ✤ ✤

There is not room enough left in this little book to tell you all that happened next; how the Wilkies really did move to Tickletakes; and — what do you think? — Great-Uncle Jeremiah went to live with Mr. Petercoo!

Great-Uncle, it turned out, had only lived at Frog's Hole because he was poor, not because he liked it; and Mr. Petercoo — why, he was a lonely old bachelor, he said; another old bachelor would be company in the evenings when the canaries were asleep. And Great-Uncle could mind the shop while Mr. Petercoo mended watches.

Next year, Robin was apprenticed to the miller; Jenny used to peep in, and see her brother, floury and happy, at work among the sacks and great millstones.

But, before this, there was an event which *must* be told!

PRINCESS MELINA

◆

A letter, with a red seal and a crown on the envelope, came to Jenny, to say that Princess Melina wished to see her, and would send a coach to fetch her to the Palace.

It was quite a long journey, and Mrs. Wilkie went too; but when they arrived, Jenny was led alone to the Princess.

The little girl saw, as in a dream, the long polished corridors, the footmen with their powdered hair, the grand ladies and gentlemen; but when at last she stood before Princess Melina, and had curtsied as she had been told to do, she found herself looking into a face so young and kind that she could not be frightened.

The Princess took Jenny's hand and drew her nearer, and asked her about the fairy gift. She told Jenny that she should wear the diamond necklace at her wedding; and she asked her whether she would like to come and live at the Palace and learn to be a little Maid of Honour.

But Jenny shook her head. She would rather stay with Mother at Tickletakes, she said.

The Princess was surprised to find that the child to whom the fairies had given pearls and diamonds, had no wish to be a grand lady.

"But you are fond of pretty things, aren't you, Jenny?" she said. "You must have been sorry to part with so many of your necklaces, though I know the money was needed. I should like to do something for you. Think — what are your wishes?"

Jenny thought. One dream had not yet come true — dear Mr. Petercoo's!

She explained about the seat in the Square, and the drinking-fountain for thirsty children.

"I wish I might pay for those things out of my money," she said; "but I don't know if there is enough, or how to do it!"

The Princess asked: "Are any necklaces yet unsold? I should like to buy some myself, if Mr. Petercoo would bring them to show me."

"There are lots of necklaces still!" said Jenny; "there's one I think the prettiest of all — blue, with emeralds and little pearls."

"Perhaps I shall buy that one!" said the Princess. "Then I would ask Mr. Petercoo to set aside some of the money, and I would write to the Mayor of your town and ask him to have your wishes carried out. I won't forget!"

Then she kissed Jenny, and said good-bye.

❊   ❊   ❊   ❊   ❊   ❊   ❊   ❊   ❊

Sure enough, the Princess did send for Mr. Petercoo, and bought necklaces for all her bridesmaids and the emeralds and aquamarines for herself.

And so, when summer evenings came again, Mr. William Petercoo, Mr. Jeremiah Titmuss, and their cronies, sat in a row on a comfortable seat by the church wall, near the new drinking-fountain, talking of old times and watching the passers-by.

The Fairy and the Elf (who was a Good Elf by now) peeped into Jenny's bedroom at Tickletakes. There stood the silver-handled chest; Claribell sat on it, wearing Jenny's old bead necklace put twice round her neck.

"I'm glad our Queen trusted Jenny with that gift!" said the Fairy.

"Yes," said the Elf; "it did bring luck, didn't it?"